Necessary Reflections

Six Short Stories

By Lee S. Holt

Necessary Reflections

© 2016 Lee S. Holt

ISBN: 978-1-61170-238-5

Book design and illustrations by Lee S. Holt

Published by:

 Robertson Publishing™
Fremont, California USA
www.RobertsonPublishing.com

Printed in the USA and UK on acid-free paper.
To purchase additional copies of this book go to:
  amazon.com
  barnesandnoble.com

For Kay Burns

Acknowledgments

I wish to thank Susan Samuels Drake for her guidance and editing throughout the process of writing these six short stories.

Love and affection always to Brenda Hill for her continuing support in all my endeavors, many thanks.

Contents

The Biggest Word 1

Caligula Rising 11

Hard Times: Heartland 21

Jalapeno Park 29

Popular Mechanics 37

She Left Him for a Woman She Hid Under Her Bed 57

About the Author 73

The Biggest Word

It was one of those heat waves. William felt listless, but he went downstairs just the same around three o'clock in the afternoon to see if there was any mail. He and his wife, Bernadette, lived in one of the single-bedroom units in the apartment building. Their flat was on the second floor in back with the manager's place downstairs.

Outside on the front porch, the sun beat down, making it hot and miserable. Running his eyes along the row of eight mailboxes, William saw some mail in his slot and took it out of the box, the metal putting a sharp burn on his fingers. Closing the screen door on the porch, he noticed a small white butterfly bumping against the doorframe. He captured it with his free hand and felt its wings beating in his loose grip before throwing it back outside. The insect fluttered momentarily near the doorsill before disappearing into the stagnant air.

William had been laid off, but figured that any day he might be getting a letter calling him back to work from Knight Ridder Newspapers. He'd been doing some handyman jobs around the apartment building for cash under the table since his unemployment had run out, but it was a fits and starts kind of thing. Oh, yeah, the manger kept saying that he was a genius every time he repaired the AC unit or one of the water heaters, every time he fixed the electricity or plumbing, but the one bringing home the bacon was Bernadette.

Climbing the stairs, he anxiously ripped open the first envelope and there it was. That's how it works. If there's mail in your mailbox, you figure it's yours. Who scrutinizes every word and line in the address window of every envelope? It was the mailman. The sonofabitch had delivered the wrong mail again.

It was another guy's mail—Mohrke. The address was somewhere down the street. Entering the kitchen, William shook the envelope and the correspondence fell out. He picked up his beer and looked over the letter. It did no harm—an honest mistake. You can always patch the envelope back together and tape it up on the row of mailboxes. It was nothing much, some news about a COLA adjustment from the Department of Veterans Affairs. The guy must have been a lifer in the service. They were telling him what he could expect to get for an increase because of his status or something.

William thought… if I'd been a lifer I could be earning money every month from the V. A., too; pull down some bennies and sit back with my feet up, maybe have more time to land a different job. He drained his beer, crumpled the can in one hand, and pitched it into the left side of the double sink. It clattered on top of the other empties.

He fanned the remaining envelopes and looked through them, and sure enough, there was another letter for this guy, Mohrke. He tossed it onto the kitchen counter. Outside of the usual junk mail, the only thing for him and his wife was the telephone bill and something about a sales seminar. From habit, he leafed through the gaudy ads.

The advertisements, when he was tired of looking at them, he dumped into a paper bag next to the back door. Bernadette wouldn't like that because she said it was relaxing for her to go over the store ads: clothes, appliances, travel stuff, when she came home from work. She said it helped her unwind. William was afraid of what she might see and want. He'd told her they better not be getting anything extra right now.

William put the telephone statement and a seminar announcement addressed to his wife in the middle of the table and got another beer out of the refrigerator. Walking around the table, he wondered how much the telephone charges would be for the month.

The bill lay there. William decided to leave it for her to open since he was the one who had been getting the mail lately—rejection letters from other newspapers that he'd sent his résumés and applications to, offering his expertise. Bernadette had said if he was able to read the newspaper before everybody else because of his managerial job in the press room, why hadn't he read about the coming layoffs? He told her that he knew all the headlines, obits, and box scores, but never ran across anything that said he was going to get axed.

The telephone jangled. "Hi," Bernadette said, "Bill?"

"Who'd you expect?" he said, with a laugh and at once he knew his voice was too high, too grating.

"What about the mail?"

"What about it?" he volleyed.

"Did it come?"

"Yeah. That sonofabitchin' mailman."

"What now?"

"We got a couple letters for some Mohrke guy—in our mailbox. You'd think the stupid mailman could read the numbers right. What's so damn hard about reading a number?"

"You get anything? I don't have too much time," she said. "I'm busy calling prospects that I met at the sales conference."

"You got some mail, plus the phone bill's all." He put the beer can down and bumped it along the edge of the tile countertop.

Her voice dropped. "Leave all of it for me, will you?"

He could tell what was going on with her. He could tell she was annoyed. His impulse was to say something like: damn it I just heard from George, our building manager, about some more work around here, or I picked up a lead from a guy that I bumped into. But it all seemed like the same old, same old thing.

"Got a minute?" he said, without really expecting much of an answer.

"I said...."

"I know what you said. You said you don't have any spare time. What's this? You can't free yourself up for a second to talk to me?" Her breath exhaled through the line and pinched at his ear. "Bernadette, you there?"

"Uh-huh."

"Listen to me, will you?"

"Bill. How long have I been listening to you? Have you been listening to yourself? I've been listening for such a damn long time. And you know what I hear? All I hear is the scratch at the end of the record. The scritch scratch. You've been playing and playing and replaying it. I won't bore

3

you with the words, let alone the sing-song of the melody. I haven't asked, pleaded, cajoled much, have I? Just get some regular work. Pull your weight. Do the decent thing—"

"Do the decent thing?"

"Listen to what I'm saying or I'll do something myself," she said.

"So now you're pushing me into some kind of corner. Is that it?"

"I've tried everything that I know. Now I think it only fair that *you* figure how we can begin to get out of this mess since *you* say you're so good at deciphering what your next employment should be with all your expertise."

"I don't know where the hell you're coming from with this attitude, Bernadette."

"Let's not fool ourselves here…"

"But you mean *me*, right?"

"Both of us. We can't afford any more slip-ups. Who knows if the newspaper will call you back. If they ever do, it could be too late." Her voice had a steel edge to it.

"What are you talking about—'could be too late'. What's up with that? I'm telling you, it'll happen any day."

"Put an application in at the post office. Then maybe at least we'd be getting our mail and not somebody else's." And she was gone with a click.

He knew what she was up to. She was sitting there with that distant look in her eyes, staring out of the office window—folded into herself as if she didn't have a bone in her body. She'd been doing it at home lately. He put a hard squeeze on the can of beer, its liquid frothed out of the top, and he slammed the receiver down.

Circling the table, he studied the envelope that held the telephone bill. This statement's both of ours, he thought. I could open it. Nothing wrong with that, I could explain I didn't get a chance to tell her that I'd already opened it before she cut me off.

He took a paring knife out of the drawer, picked up the envelope, and slit it open along one edge. I could pay this one. I still got a few bucks left over from one of our two savings accounts that I cleaned out.

The telephone bill spilled out onto the table, face down. He pulled out a chair and sat there with the statement in front of him.

She would bring it up tonight—how many places had he applied to? Had he gone to the library to check all the help-wanted ads in every newspaper? That way she had about her—asking, pressing, probing. What had he found online?

Slipping the knife blade under the bill, he flipped the statement face up. There was a short list of local calls for the month. He studied them and then moved to the long distance. An entry to Santa Monica, made around midnight last weekend? That had to be a mistake. He scratched around through the kitchen drawers until he found a pencil and circled the number. Now they were getting wrong billing from the phone company along with other people's mail and it pissed him off. He would call the Santa Monica phone number, find out who's it was so he could yell at the phone company—show them how screwed up and incompetent their people were.

He grabbed the telephone and punched in the numbers. The other end rang a long time before somebody picked it up. "Well hallo there," some guy's sugary voice said. The warm tone of the words oozed over the line.

William hadn't thought much about how he was going to approach it up until then. He took a sip of beer and could only manage, "What's the time out there?"

With abruptness, the timbre of the man's voice changed. "What? Almost three thirty. Who's this? Whadya want? This is a private line."

"Some information."

"What about—a seminar? Because you've reached Armstrong Sales Incorporated."

"Yeah. Yeah, that's it, about a seminar. Give me some information on that."

William studied the brochure that was addressed to Bernadette. The front cover blared: *Reach Your Full Sales Potential: Be a Ten by Using John Armstrong's Direct Sales Methodology.*

"This line's for personal calls only. You're supposed to call reservations about the next class session. You got that number?" the voice on the other end of the line instructed.

William's mouth twisted as he examined the picture on the front of the brochure showing the smirking sales professional, relaxed, posing in front of a marina, white smile set off by his deep Southern California tan.

"Yeah. I've got your number, all right."

"Call Veronica. She'll give you all the particulars and send an announcement of our next presentation out to you."

Through the phone line William heard the laugh of some woman in Santa Monica. He heard Armstrong signing off. He heard a roaring like the ocean in his ear. The sonofabitchin' address and phone number on the brochure was all wrong—the mail was supposed to have been sent to Bernadette's office, not to their apartment.

William dropped the receiver on the counter, scooped up Mohrke's letters, and turned on the garbage disposal. He fed the government letter into the whirring blades. His fingers inched closer and closer to the drain, to the spinning air, just below the black rubber flaps.

The dark cavity was a Siren's call to him. That'd do it. Bernadette would have to see what he was going through—everything would be laid bare.

The disposal jammed when he shoved the second envelope into the hole. He tore himself away and flipped off the switch, leaned against the cool counter tile, sweating hard. A beeping tone pulsed from the forgotten telephone receiver, matching his pounding heart. He slammed the phone into the cradle, grabbed a dish towel, and wiped his forehead, around his eyes. He picked up his beer and stumbled out of the kitchen.

The place felt hotter than ever. In the living room, William turned on the TV and sank into the old brown couch that he and Bernadette had reupholstered and stared at a game show where stupid people acting stupid were winning thousands of dollars. The latest newscast spewed out the winning lottery numbers. More money to be won by blacking out boxes with cheap pencil stubs, a brainless reflex. Where was his break? Where was his win?

He dug at the loose threads on the arm of the sofa with his ring finger and then stood up. He walked over to the window and watched the tar melt on the roof of the adjacent building. The small mirror on the wall caught his reflection. A middle-aged image stared back at him. Thinning uncombed hair, worn t-shirt, and a three-day beard met his gaze.

His wife's words spiraled back to him. He had to figure something out. This Mohrke guy seemed to have cracked the riddle. He'd done something right. The neighborhood was a transition area: a mix of houses and apartments. Mohrke might actually own one of those houses.

William thought that perhaps he should have stayed in like Mohrke—gotten something from Uncle Sam instead of always being a clown, just in it to have fun. Maybe he could have studied to become some kind of an engineer. He couldn't screw this Mohrke guy, couldn't hang him out to dry, leave him twisting in the wind.

In the kitchen, he rummaged around until he found a screwdriver and wrench. With both hands, he pulled out the drying rack for dishes, detergents, and cleaning items from under the sink. He unplugged the garbage disposal, released the mount ring, and tried to pick out the fragments of paper.

His shoulder and hip hurt. He drew blood on one knuckle. The pieces of paper that emerged were black and greasy. He spread them out on the kitchen table.

An hour later, Bernadette came in the front door and called, "Bill? You here?" She turned on the living room lamp and entered the kitchen to find him sitting at the table surrounded by cans of cleansers, food waste, and the garbage disposal. With a pair of tweezers and a plastic magnifying glass, William was attempting to piece together the scraps of paper from the disposal.

"Bill, what the hell! God damn it, Bill, what's going on? What the hell's happened?" Her dark eyebrows squeezed down in a frown.

"Something happened?" He raised his head, frowning.

She saw the torn telephone envelope and slumped into the chair opposite him, waited.

"Is that the telephone bill?" she said.

His eyes met hers. "What difference would it make? Please tell me the difference, Bernadette." He picked up the screwdriver. It glinted in the light with its smudge of blood. "I broke the corner of the screwdriver on the disposal," he said, with a tone of self-discovery.

Bernadette folded her arms. William saw her deep décolletage heave as her eyes darted from side to side. She spotted the dried blood on his hand. "Hold on..."

"I've been holding on. All's I've been doing. The time is for doing, now."

"For God's sake..." Bernadette winced.

He laid the screwdriver down in front of him and studied her for a long time before bringing his hands up. He interlaced his fingers, resting his elbows on the table. She drew back in her chair with a bewildered look etched across her face.

A hotness spread over him. His face burned like the tar on the roofs. A light shaking began to run through him. His mind searched for a way out of the labyrinth of his own making. He remembered seeing the *Free Shopper* flyer advertisement for a part-time job delivering merchandise for Rite Price Hardware. He didn't know if the job would be good enough for her; he hoped it might be good enough.

The pieces, of this mess about him finding work, were blowing up, new chunks hitting him faster than he could label them: the mail; Bernadette changing—everything.

"You and me... figured I knew... things. Guess I don't. Don't know what the hell this is all about anymore. Can you believe it?"

"What do you mean?" she said. "I know what I believed once—believed in us, both of us working together. This path is so convoluted now that I don't know whether I'm coming or going, whether we're making it or not, whether either of us thinks we're worth it."

"I'm just talking about things, just saying about how I figured things were and how they are now. Different, it's all different now. Some mail here, some mail there—changes this whole place—us," he said, gazing around the room.

She countered, "Some mail? Here? There? There's a lot more to it than that. I know what's happened. I've gone from believing in you, to believing your excuses, to not being able to believe anything that you tell me. What am I supposed to do? Tell me. Just what am I supposed to do?"

William held up his hand for her to stop. "I know."

She said, "I can't take any more. I just can't. It's breaking me—"

"I'm fixing it tomorrow. There's an ad in the *Shopper* for a Rite Price Hardware delivery job."

"Tomorrow? It's been tomorrow with you—with—us for almost a year now..."

"One step at a time's all I need. I'm applying for it tomorrow, early. Give me a break here. That's all I'm asking, Bernadette. I'm asking you." His hand shook with a careless motion at the debris surrounding them. "I opened up this Mohrke guy's letter. I was… I don't know what… I stuffed it down the disposal. Not something I'm proud of, not something I'd let anybody know but you."

Her eyes flitted to the mail on the table. She uncovered the telephone bill and seminar brochure, swept them into her lap while keeping her eyes on her husband. "Tomorrow then—something's got to give one way or the other, same as this damn stifling heat, for better or worse."

"No more worse, only better."

"And this?" she said, gesturing to the shredded paper in front of her husband.

The kitchen wall clock told William that the sun was setting in Santa Monica. Again, the ocean crashed in his head. "I'll do something with it. I just don't know what… What the hell do I know? Should I go over and tell him that it got destroyed by accident? Stuff gets destroyed by accident. We don't mean it to, but it does. Consequences aren't always thought of beforehand. We slip up. I've slipped up—a lot."

"I never wanted this, Bill, never. Maybe if we hadn't lost our way…"

"No, no. If I hadn't lost my job…"

"The biggest word in the world…"

"What's that?" Bill said.

"If."

Bernadette rose from the table and opened the window in the kitchen to let in the evening breeze. William sat rigid. She began making baloney and cheese sandwiches on white bread. She got out some sour pickles and potato chips. With a deliberate movement she laid each slice of the meat and cheese on the bread, lining them up, nudging them into place.

William resumed assembling bits of the letters, pushing threads of paper around with a pencil beneath the overhead light. Bernadette picked up the brochure, studied the picture of Armstrong, and tore it in half before throwing it in the trash.

When they finished eating, she cleared the table. William brought their plates over to the garbage container and scraped them off. He bent down to snatch a bit of curled gold plastic from the cheese wrapper off the floor and leaned close to her.

With an audible sigh she shifted her weight, but didn't move away from him. "I can't even wash the dishes until you put the sink back together." Her voice cracked.

He pushed his head against his wife's side and heard her heart drumming on the other side of her cotton blouse. He feels again the butterfly's wings fluttering against his hand, their staccato beat.

In his mind he imagines the butterfly returning, beating its wings against the screen: a small white offering to Bernadette's dim silhouette standing behind the screen door. He waits, hoping that it might be enough.

Caligula Rising

The thin boy stood next to a tall woman with graying hair. With both hands, he gripped the metal railing overlooking the central atrium in a large nondescript mall, watching the escalators and elevators move to the upper and lower floors. "How long do we have to wait?" The youngster looked up at the woman.

"I don't know, my little prince. Let's watch the people while we do." The woman said.

"Will I know her?"

"Of course you'll know her. Everybody knows their mother, I suppose."

"I could watch the people on the escalators and in the elevators forever. Where are they going? Where are they coming from? Some hold small packages, others don't. See the way that man is dressed? Have you ever seen anyone dressed like that? Who would dress like that?" Then the boy hunched his shoulders, leaning forward so he could see as many of the people as possible as they glided up and down.

"I'm sure your mother will come soon." The woman placed her hand on the railing next to his.

"I suppose." The boy shifted from one foot to the other and brushed back a lock of wild dark hair hanging over his forehead.

Among the people that they watched, one couple rose on the escalator, chatting amicably as they went by. The woman was dressed in a kaleidoscope of colors, while the man's clothes were a single shade of gray. "Can you hear what they're saying?" The woman tilted her head.

"Not clearly, something about something or other. They're acting happy. Maybe they're here to buy something for someone—maybe a birthday present." The boy's eyes brightened and he inched closer to the woman.

"That's probably it," the woman said. "Or perhaps clothes for school. School will be soon starting, I would imagine. When you get older, like me, you don't keep track of the school year. Teachers, parents, and students know exactly what dates to mark on the calendar. To others, it's not that important. My mother used to say, 'Maybelle, it's up to you to remind me about your school days because I'm too busy to keep track of everything. So, you must take care of it.' And I agree."

"I like the Romans," the child volunteered, referring to school. "I know a lot of the emperor's names and how bad they were."

Maybelle said, "Not all of them were so terrible, I guess. It was a different time back then. A lot of people did atrocious things to one another. I liked their costumes—their clothes, when I was a girl, about your age—eight or nine, I suppose."

An elderly woman with white hair and furrowed brow approached them. She breathed heavily and rocked from side to side as though her hips hurt. She wore several layers of mismatched clothing with a loosened orange scarf and yellow gloves peeking out of her coat pockets.

"Is this the home furnishings floor? Seems I've been looking for the Home Furnishings Department for so long. Why, you two look just like an aunt and nephew, I say. There's some resemblance, in the eyes. Yes, I can see it in the eyes and across the brow." The woman touched her eyebrows and the bridge of her nose.

"Such a funny thing to say, but thank you; I don't know if the home furnishings are on this level. Seems we've just arrived. There should be a directory over by the foyer." Maybelle gestured toward one of the entryways.

"Maybe I'll try that. I haven't had much luck talking to people. They all seem to be wrapped up in their own thoughts—and trying to get somewhere or another."

"Maybe these two men coming toward us will know—" Maybelle said.

Two glowering men approached. They hunched their shoulders, eyes darting from side to side. The larger of the two, swathed in a great coarse-knit cloak, padded ahead of a younger man dressed in leather with fur trim.

"Keep your eyes sharp, thrall," he whispered.

"Yes, sir," the younger man said, "whatever you wish."

The two groups measured each other.

"If they bleed and die, they're not demons," the man said.

"Sir, we've come to know. Remember? They're the same as us, although they are peculiar and different..." The young man stepped forward.

The small boy moved away from the railing, "Hello, I'm Pic, where have you been? Where are you going? Did you see my mother?"

"We're on our way somewhere," the older man's mouth turned down.

The young man said, "Going somewhere that will be on our way..."

"Oh," Maybelle said, drawing away from them. "You'd better, then, I suppose."

"I guess," the youth said, "If my master deems it so."

"How funny, such a way of couching it." Maybelle smiled.

"Couch, how's that?" The older man frowned. "Lurking? An ambush?"

"Not couch in that sense, master."

"I'll couch this..." The older man's right hand slipped under his garment and he touched an empty scabbard. He raised his left hand, fist clenched.

The thrall cleared his throat and tugged at the man's cloak. The larger man wavered, grunted, and wiped his sleeve across his face.

The elderly woman's eyes widened and her voice quivered. "I'll just be going into this store to see if they can help me..." She hobbled away as fast as she could, glancing over her shoulder.

The two men moved closer to Pic and Maybelle. Pic stepped aside. The men brushed past and trudged down the concourse.

Pic turned and pointed toward the store entrance. "What's that lady doing?"

The elderly woman hesitated at the doorway and shuffled her feet forward. Staring into the interior, she adjusted her forward progress an inch at a time. After several moments of staring down at her shoes and then looking up, as if waiting for something, she finally stepped through the entryway.

The situation struck Pic and he looked up at Maybelle. "Are you waiting, too?"

"Am I, my little prince? Maybe I am—I really couldn't say. It doesn't seem as though I am, yet I might be. I'm sure I will know later, if not sooner, but for now let's go sit down in those seats and I'll think about matters. Things will be easier if we sit down and rest a bit," she said, gesturing at the seating area further along the concourse. "We will do something. We won't do anything."

The two of them sat down to rest. Maybelle took one shoe off and rubbed her foot. "That's much better."

"It is easier, I suppose." Pic said.

"In some ways," Maybelle said. "But, not all ways."

"So, not always?" Pic turned around in his seat to get a better look whenever he saw other people pass by.

"That is true," Maybelle replaced her shoe.

Pic sprang up. "Like the Roman emperors not always being bad. The Emperor Claudius did good things, but then there was Tiberius and his adopted son, Germanicus. I read that the Roman Empire lasted for more than five hundred years; they had dynasties just like in the Orient. There was even a year of four emperors..." After a moment, as though he was mulling over a problem, he said, "Do you think it ever gets dark?"

"Can you tell if it does?" Maybelle looked up.

"The light stays the same... It always has," Pic said.

"Yes, maybe so, I suppose that is how it is."

"I wish my mother was here."

"She will find you if she is, I'm sure. You keep watching for her. This is a good spot. We can see everyone that comes by and keep an eye on the escalators and elevators from here. I'm just going to rest my eyes for a minute..." Maybelle's eyelids fluttered closed.

Pic crossed and uncrossed his legs. He tugged at his double socks on each leg. He sat forward watching a woman rising in a glass elevator. She stared straight ahead, a totem, seemingly uninterested in her surroundings. He slid back, studying a few people getting off the escalator. Presently he fell asleep in his chair.

* * *

Pic woke with a start, expecting to be somewhere else, yet his surroundings seemed to be exactly as they should be. Maybelle lounged in the chair next to him, watching people on the escalators. Turning her attention to him, she said, "I wondered how long you'd nap, my fine fellow."

A faint jangling from a set of bells echoed along the concourse. A curly-haired, squat man, pushing a three-wheel cart, approached them. The cart had bright, colored signs plastered all over it publicizing ice cream and popsicles. The man wore white crisp-starched pants and shirt. There was a small cap set at a jaunty angle on his head.

"Ice cream, here!" the man called out. "Name's Kayak. What'll it be? Ice cream? Here we go, have one of these."

He opened one lid on the top of the small cart, reached in and pulled out an Eskimo Pie ice cream bar. "No? How 'bout one of these?" He put the ice cream back, opened a second lid, and held up a red popsicle. "How 'bout one of these raspberry ones, then?"

Pic said, "But I don't have any money…"

"No? Not to worry, you can pay me tomorrow, then," Kayak exclaimed.

"When my mother comes?"

"No, whenever you can. Not to worry, my little lad. Not to worry. Our time today is all too short to worry over such trivial matters. Tomorrows are inconsequential. Today is all that counts. Live in the moment, nothing else. Do what you do better than what you do and do everything else in the here and now."

Maybelle rose and came close to the ice cream cart, studying the signage. "I see no posted prices…"

"No, no prices—a mere meaningless token of a barter, an illusion of worth, the nonsensical pronouncement of the irrelevant." Kayak said.

Maybelle said, "Then I want my favorite flavor—in all of the world, it's the best flavor. And I would imagine that you have never even heard of it, my good man. I want a Blue Moon ice cream cone."

The man sunk his hand into the well of the cart and pulled out a huge scoop of Blue Moon ice cream, pounded it into a waffle cone and held it aloft. "No, not a problem, here it is, madam, see? And what for you now, my little man? No, you'll want Tinutong na bigas, or Basashi—some of my other bests."

"Maybe just vanilla…" Pic said, as once more, the older man and his young companion approached.

Maybelle said, "They must be out for a walk…"

"Here we are then." The younger man glanced around.

"Here we are then." The older man winced.

"We are here." The younger man nodded his approval.

"Yes, we are here." The older man ground his teeth.

"Look at these fine people," the young man said. "They seem so busy. They seem so happy. Because they seem so, I might want to buy this ice cream business."

"This business, my friend, cannot be for sale," Kayak said, turning to them.

"Any business can be bought or sold for the right price," the young man insisted.

"No. Merely a pronouncement of the irrelevant—a mere gesture of words spoken, an illusion of meaning," Kayak chuckled.

The young man turned to his associate, "One must take advantage of a disadvantage if it is advantageous to one, do you see?"

"Ah, I think so, but I have never been any good with anything." The old man's shoulders sagged.

"Exactly! Which makes you always not good at anything, and it is superior to be an *Always* rather than a *Never*."

"I'm beginning to comprehend what you're saying," the older man's expression brightened.

"Precisely."

"In a matter such as this, time is of the essence, as the essence of time is the essence."

"Indeed."

"Therefore, we shall conclude. We shall end, but, not the end-game. We will cease—"

"But not desist?" The older man knit his brow.

"We shall go about, we shall circle around, we shall approach from another position, we will—"

"Bide our time?" The older man slouched.

"Absolutely, we shall speak of it another time, bite our tongues, wait our chance, my friends." The young man addressed both his companion and Kayak.

"Surely—we'll adjourn for the moment." The older man bowed slightly and swept his arm before him.

"Take notes. Put them into the minutes. Prepare them for tomorrow." The young man checked his wrist as though he was wearing a wristwatch.

"Yes sir." The older man came to attention.

"Now is the time we must discuss where we are with these things—matters of importance—the markets rise, the markets fall."

"—and other aspirations as well," the older man offered.

"—solid, very solid, insight."

"Thank you—I thought—a different perspective…"

"That's what I'm looking for—what the board is looking for—for that matter and that's what matters with these matters."

"Yes, solid matters, sir. Solid ground—matters."

"Grounded on solid ground," the young man said. "Until the 'morrow, then. Until the bell tolls, when the clapper strikes. The following day. As in the day that follows the night." He stepped backward.

Kayak reiterated. "No. Tomorrows are inconsequential. Today is all that counts. We live in the moment, meaning less than a minute, nothing else. Do what you do better, and do everything else in the here and now."

The young man turned with a flourish, "I have places to go, things to do, people to meet, hands to shake, babies to kiss. So off we go. Come along old man."

The two men remained. They stepped aside and began a discussion in low tones.

"Since we are here, where we're at, I also want to discuss some opportunities that I have in mind—with you in mind." the young man said.

"By all means, by all means." The older man became intent.

"I have ideas that, generally speaking, will apply to our means."

"All of our means?" The older man's brow furrowed.

"The mean of our means in the least."

"Quite."

"If not all, then some. If not some, then all, I mean." The young man walked down the concourse, with the older man one step behind, gesturing with his hands, as if he were painting a vast picture for his older companion.

Without handing the ice cream cone to Maybelle, Kayak raised one eyebrow. "May I?" he said, indicating that he was going to return the ice cream to the tub.

"Of course," Maybelle said. "We both understand each other from top to bottom."

He replaced the Blue Moon ice cream into the well of his cart and clapped his hands. "That went so well! An absolute stunning success! Euphrosyne of the Charities! If nothing else."

The elderly woman reappeared at the store entrance. She stared at her feet for a moment, raised her head, and shuffled her feet forward a few inches before repeating the process over and over.

"I'll see if she needs help," Maybelle said.

Kayak began wiping off his ice cream cart and rearranging the signs, placing them upside down. Then, from one side of the pushcart, he stretched across on his stomach, so he could read the upside-down words on the opposite side of the cart.

Pic took up his position at the rail, leaning forward, and waited for people to appear in the elevators. He counted the number of individuals rising against the number descending.

Maybelle helped the elderly woman along the concourse, adjusting one of her garments, tucking one glove deeper into her pocket.

"You know, that wasn't home furnishings after all. I thought it was because I believe that I had a very nice nap in there. I wonder what department that was..." the old woman said.

Maybelle patted the woman's hand as they walked toward Pic. An escalator was nearby. Maybelle walked to the edge of the moving stairs where the muffled thump, thump, thump of the mechanism resounded.

Pic's breath caught in his throat at the sight of the two women so close to the emerging steps. Were they leaving? Why would they want to leave? Where would they go? He was about to run toward them when he caught a flutter of garment out of the corner of his eye. He twisted around. A man wearing a tunic was rising in an elevator. He passed Pic without acknowledgment, the same as others had done before. An expression of recognition spread across Pic's face. He turned toward Maybelle hoping to get her attention.

Pic's words emerged garbled. He pointed and tried again as the man moved upward. "Caligula! It's Caligula, rising!" His shout echoed through the immense space.

From somewhere down below in the vast mall a voice called, "Our star!"

A beautiful woman, sitting on the opposite side of the atrium, pivoted toward Pic and sprang to her feet, dropping her handkerchief to the floor. With a wild expression she clasped her fist to her mouth, biting her knuckle. Pic stared across the gulf between them. A realization formed in him, although he was unable to attach a word to it.

Hard Times: Heartland

With a lunge, the morning tore off its dark harness and pulled the blood-red disk up over the low hills in the East. It would be another merciless, hot day. A thin shard of the sunlight ricocheted off the top of the barn, and then zigzagged its way down to the trees, across the scraggly corn, and through the blistered oats. The barn threw up a shadow as if to protect itself from the onslaught and waited out the morning hours.

Crossing the barren ground, the young man walked with long strides from the shadow of the corn crib into the intense light, leaving ashen-gray clouds of dust hanging in the still air before they settled back down to earth as though he had disturbed them from their feeding. He wiped his neck with his handkerchief, mounted the low back porch, and entered the kitchen of the farmhouse.

As he washed-up, the only sound in the room came from the narrow ribbon of water spiraling from the faucet and splashing into the chipped enameled sink. He wiped his hands and gazed out of the window.

The woman sat, bent at the table, smoothing out a wrinkle in the oil cloth that clung to the hard surface. She ran her fingers along its ridge as a mother might straighten her child's unruly hair, pressing it down, and telling it to stay in place.

The farmer hung the towel on a peg, pulled up a chair and sat down hard. "You slept on the hall floor last night."

"Yes—it was cooler there by the upstairs window," she said, studying his large hands and sunburned throat.

"Cooler?"

"The center hall is always a bit cooler, when it's hot." She lowered her eyes.

"Twenty-eight days of clouds chalking the evening sky—and each night they're erased by some fiendish devil to show a cleaned slate in the morning light. Not a hint of moisture wrapped in them. It couldn't be cooler *a bit* in the center hall."

"It was," she countered.

"It'll rain before this day is through, I swear to God it will." He frowned and stared past her toward the narrow staircase in the hallway. He clenched his fist. She rose, turned to the stove, and began ladling a meager bit of chipped beef and gravy from skillet to plate.

"Why did you unlatch the shutters, there?" He nodded toward the open window. "It's already hazed over, and the stable flies are beginning to bite. I'm telling you, rain is on its way. That damn tin thermometer's streak of red climbing toward the back porch rafters has to break, has to give up its senseless rise and run back down—"

"Mother would've called this heat wave a 'kettle boiler.' All I'm praying for is a breeze to take the smell of silage and dry burdock out of our clothes," she said.

A vacant expression overcame her and she drifted away, lost in thought, gazing out of the door toward the looming barn, before setting his plate in front of him with as much interest as an apple might have in falling from a tree.

"I'll have to admit," he said, "the crops in the field need a drink even more than the stock. There's still some mud water trickling in the lower creek for the cattle to get to. I'll have to move that wagonload of hay into the barn when it does rain, though."

They ate their midday meal in silence. The farmer wiped his plate clean with a slice of bread. He studied his wife's lowered head with her long dark hair tied back, hoping to catch her attention if she looked up. He said, "I take it that you're still getting eggs from the chickens."

"A few," was all she offered in way of reply.

"We may be able to trade them with the Adamson family for some of their canned vegetables."

The woman nodded, collected their plates and tableware, and scraped what few bits of food remained into the hog's slop bucket for later. She reminded herself that there were a few garments pinned to the clothesline in the backyard, and the upstairs hall window needed to be shut in case the flat pale sky actually held some wetness.

After her husband returned to his chores, she remained seated at the kitchen table holding to her breast a child's toy top that she had made nearly two years ago from an empty sewing spindle. The woman ran her fingers over the rough thread wrapped around the blue shank. Again and again she wound the string tight before letting it unravel, picturing her husband quickly pull the string to set the top careening across the hardwood floor, rousing their son's laughter as the toy skittered and wobbled before falling, ready to be rewound.

Although not yet thirty years old, the farmer's face was drawn and creased from the weather, long hours in the fields, and worry. He leaned against the edge of the corrugated stock tank and rolled a cigarette. There had been rumors of some farmers blocking roads so no food would get to market. They hoped to boycott the processing plants and canneries by withholding their produce, not even letting neighbors through to sell their harvest. Others, further west, had been burning grain in their stoves because the grain elevators were overflowing with unsold oats and wheat. Milk was being dumped on the roads the way alcohol had been during Prohibition. The hard times of the Depression were making it impossible to survive, and no one seemed to have any idea how to fix what was wrong with the country; those that might seemed unwilling to act.

He had worked every summer on his uncle's farm and spent long hours studying agriculture in school. Farming, he had imagined, would provide more freedom to be his own man, relying on hard work and personal fortitude. Instead, he was overwhelmed with the difficulties battering him from all sides—being required to be a juggler—compelled to keep the pins in the air. He was no juggler.

The woman went outside and took the sheets and pillowcases off the clothesline as the summer afternoon brought black, parrot-tulip clouds rearing in the sky. She recalled how she had hated washing out diapers. Now her heart wrenched at the void, at the loss of small cotton diapers next to the bed sheets and large denim shirts. After bringing the clothes inside, the woman climbed the stairs and closed the hallway window.

An hour later, thunder rolled tight along a line of timber near the horizon. Stale air rose and slinked away. On the back porch, the farmer scrutinized the thermometer. The temperature had dropped twenty degrees in the last ten minutes as frenzied clouds stampeded toward the farm. The shutters on the kitchen window began to pick up the swelling rhythm of the wind, straining to break free and search for a more suitable home.

"I'll hitch up the mule and bring in the hay; lucky to have it," he said as she moved close to the back door.

A frown stitched his wife's brow and she caught her breath. "Lucky, lucky?" She turned, facing him. "What is it that you call luck, Ephrem? I'd like to know—"

"What I meant, Margaret, was to be thankful for being here, on the Knox farm. Renting the place at this time of year—after I had already planted the crops at the old place. These are hard times and F.D.R.'s New Deal is slow in coming to tenant farmers like us."

"How can you do that? Talk of *luck* with that in my sight?" Her glower deepened as she looked at the wagon standing before the barn door.

"You know the wagon had to be kept when we came to this farm. Last year's crop money wasn't enough to buy another." He sighed. "You and I had to carry our belongings in something when we moved."

"Haven't I pleaded with you? Get it out of my sight! Destroy the thing! How can you keep it, look at it, touch it with hands that have touched me, knowing what it has done?"

"It was an accident—those things are accidents. There is no answer found in them. I'll clear this place of it as soon as the corn goes to mill in the fall, if the market has returned. I promise. I swear."

"You swear, as demanding it to rain a few moments ago, I suppose." She spat the words across the empty space between them.

The kitchen's screen door bumped against the doorjamb on the freshening wind. He glanced toward the barn.

"I see your stare," she said. "I can see you eyeing that thing."

He opened the kitchen door and stepped back inside. "I have to get it into the bay of the barn, now!"

"The beast!" Her voice rose in anguish, to match his height. "That devil thing took my first born from me. Killing our son with its cloven wheels while you rode it! I feel it here!" Margaret pounded her chest. "Ephrem, I still see you carry our son, stumble to the back porch, sink to your knees with him limp in your arms. And yet you have the gall leaving me to go to that wagon!"

"The storm is almost on us. It's spilling across the upper pasture now!" His anxious eyes darted to the hilltop, then back at her.

She pressed herself against the window sill, watched the boiling thunderheads. Lightning licked and crackled across their bellies. "Your life is of this dried clay—nothing more. You will seek to break it all your days, if I know anything about you—trying to draw it into you, as though it could be made a part of you, your souls tightly joining each other. You could have chosen another path," she said. "You had the chance to help out my father in his feed and grain store."

He lowered his head, cleaning one fingernail with another. "You agreed with what I chose to do. You agreed. And in these times, at least we have food, unlike some."

"Yes, I agreed, then, but not for our son's lifetime, not for such a short fragile lifetime: I didn't bear him just to bury him!"

"You don't care to know of the soil's hold on me. You have never joined me out there, even before that day—to hear the earth parting its way before the steel blade of the plow, or to look down on this house set into the hillside, among crowns of locust and oak, garnering in the songs of the birds as they cloister together."

"Join you? Join you where? You mean, out on that mound of kiln-dried crust you dare call a field, beneath the broiling sun?"

"See, you've made your mind up as to what you *think* it's like, not having taken the time or made the effort. I'm going now. Can't you hear the rain striking the roof?" Flies hung embedded on the door's metal mesh. He gripped the door handle and turned back toward her: "I regret what I said—about not making an effort. I know you have."

Rain rose on each gust of wind making dust explode into rings as it splattered into the ground. She said, "My torment is still unknown to you. That pain which hurts the most. How I push against it, day and night. You—you return from the field at sunset to rest. I don't rest against its relentless madness day or night."

25

"And still you won't speak to me about it. I tell you, Margaret, keeping it to yourself, nursing it, letting no one else near it as a river otter defends her pups—"

"And if I did speak of it again as I've tried to, what then?"

He rested his forearm against the door frame and pressed his forehead into his shirt sleeve. "Then I would listen to the plaint in your heart, and try to—"

"And try to change it, as you try to change everything, try to fence it, reap it, lay it low, so it will be flattened and smoothed, to be tramped upon without thorny intrusion."

"Damn! You see only what you want to see, I swear, Margaret. You should consider the land from beyond this fortress of yours. This prison you have built. Consider each season's passage: to sow, cultivate, harvest, and renew. The world is flourishing out there, moving on, and not clinging to the past."

"Nor does the world blot out the past as you would have it. Yes, alive as you say, but also conscious of history and remembrance of what has gone on before—its roots," she said.

He moved to the back porch, looking at her from the opposite side of the screen door. "After this storm moves through, we'll walk those pastures and fields—then you'll see this land around you. I promise that it cannot but make you tell me that this land can be a contract, holding us…"

She scowled at him, not moving. He left with a heavy tread over the porch, down the step, and across the yard, melding into the rain, becoming a gray silhouette.

She grasped the door and held it tight against the buffeting of the storm as the shutters on the kitchen window broke loose and pounded against the clapboard siding. "I don't want to see your vision," she said, "if that feral ground is the only thing to find out there."

The wagon, with its burden, moved slowly into the shelter of the barn. The silhouette climbed down and stood beside it, a signature in the corner of the open door frame, the curtain of rain separating the two worlds of man and woman.

"How alike they are: that wagon, that man—clumped together, angular, shedding the water," she mused, "leaving sodden stains upon the raw heartwood floor."

She thrust the screen door open against the fury of the storm, "You two—keep to yourselves—keep to your own out there!"

Oblivious to the rain streaming down his face, Ephrem grasped the back of his neck with one hand and stared skyward, imagining the small country graveyard with the sun-washed headstone. His failure filled his being. Now, he and Margaret didn't have the means to travel the twenty miles to the tiny plot in the Orth Road Cemetery on the hill overlooking the broad plain where their son was buried. Distance had barred them from their custodial craving and had left them helpless in mourning.

Ephrem struggled toward the house from the barn. He leaned into the brunt of the gale and attempted to close the kitchen shutters pummeling the house. The maelstrom slashed at his face. Margaret ran out of the house into the howling wind. As they grappled to latch the banging shutters, their eyes met. He put his arm around her shoulder as he reached for the flange. She leaned into him. Wrenching their child's toy from her apron pocket, she pushed the spindle through the eye bolt, clasping the shutters together. Exhausted, they made their way through the deluge into the house.

Margaret closed the door and switched on the single overhead light, trying to dislodge the darkness. She shuddered. Ephrem took his jacket off and covered her shoulders with it. Margaret caught the smell of farm animal and crop. Other scents rose to meet her. The jacket was soaked with an entire world, an entire life, a lifetime of seasons coming and going—part of *Continuum*. She became aware of a sensation, apart from being numb, and felt a heaviness lifting like drenched grass rising again on the wind after a cleansing thunderstorm.

Jalapeno Park

The sun shone through the summer foliage, dappling the sidewalk and grass of the city park. Arthur Donamann sat beneath three large palm trees and checked his wristwatch. He drummed his fingers near the edge of an open checkerboard on the small concrete table in front of him and scrutinized the people strolling, cycling, and jogging along the nearby path.

"This park bench is no place for a man of my age to linger over for so long. Come on will ya..." Arthur said to himself. "People have died waitin' for less."

Footsteps shuffled along the path behind him. Arthur turned his arthritic shoulder slightly to one side so that he could launch his reproach at the earliest opportunity.

"Where in the hell have ya been, for chrissake, Timmy? Ya know we start on the hour. By my watch, it's past the hour. That's the agreement, on the hour, not one minute past the hour or anything else past the hour. Ya wouldn't have missed starting your act, would ya? I never missed going on stage, but a few times in my career. And I was only a 'hoofer' don't ya know, not a 'piano man' like you. Ya shoulda learned somethin' from bein' in show business for more than sixty years, goddammnit. Our word is our bond, Timothy." Arthur's shoulders slumped. "But I'm not upset, ya musta had somethin' far more important than our game to hold ya up for so long."

Timothy Thornten sat down with a deep sigh. "Sorry, Artie, I had a doctor's appointment, and the lady before me took longer than expected. You know how some 'stars' have to hog the spotlight, explain every little detail, every little twitch and schmitch. I'm telling you, I think some of them make it their life's work." Timothy wiped his neck with his handkerchief and glanced at the checkerboard.

"Another doctor's appointment—for chrissake, stay away from that doctor of yours, will ya. I never go ta see a doctor—ya go ta the doctor, you'll *need* ta go ta the doctor—it's written," Arthur said.

"What, it's written? Show me where it's written. Nothing's written like that, Artie. You don't feel good, you go to a doctor. Your tooth hurts, you go to a dentist; your crotch aches, you go to a—"

"You're making my arse ache with your drivel," Arthur said.

"And you believe too much in your own drivel, not real reasons."

"I believe what I believe and I'm the better for it." Arthur scratched the side of his nose with his forefinger.

"Maybe you'd be better for it if you paid more attention concerning yourself. Shave more often. You're looking like one of these grizzled beach bums around here with your ratty baseball cap and your hair sticking out all over."

"And look who's talkin' with your ugly Bermuda shorts, black socks with garters almost ta your knees, and white shoes."

"Weren't you ever told to clean up, to see a doctor?"

"The only cleaning up I'm gonna do is jumping your checkers, Timmy."

"My nephew, the doctor, is a good doctor. He went through college in five years—a little long, maybe. But he went through med school in only six."

"I'm tellin' ya, Timmy, don't keep runnin' ta that doctor of yours. Don't make it your life's work, OK? Now the board's all ready ta go, so start the damn game."

"All right, I'm starting already. It's just that I've been having this tightness right here." Tim rubbed the left side of his chest.

"Tightness, schmightness." Arthur studied Tim's move.

"Maybe Jimmy BelAire should have seen his doctor more often," Tim said.

"Jimmy BelAire should've seen the handwriting on the wall. I never saw a guy hang around so long after he was washed up."

"He was a good bandleader, Artie. He gave you some breaks along the way."

"Breaks, schmeaks. I didn't need no favors from nobody. Especially little dinky Jimmy BelAire—figured he knew it all just because he had a hot sound for a few years there, back in the Fifties."

"He caught the pulse, all right. He knew what the people wanted."

"And he thought he knew more than any of us, including your pill-pushing doctor."

"He kicked off just like that." Tim snapped his fingers. "Walks out to his pool, puts his hands on his hips, draws in a big breath of air and keels over. Ker plunk."

"How in the hell do ya know that's how he went? You there?" Arthur put his left hand on his knee, preparing to make his first move.

"I heard, I heard. Saw it in *Variety* or somewhere, I think. Kicked off just like that. What a star—damn shame to lose such a talent. And he was so young."

"Young? He was eighty-three, Timmy. The man was eighty-three years old. A year younger than you, for chrissake." Arthur moved his first checker.

"But to leave behind a widow, the likes of Dolly LaFarge, Artie."

"It's true. Now there's a widow—va-va-voom. Such va-va's, I'm tellin' ya—"

"To see all of Dolly LaFarge, every day—I wouldn't need to see a doctor…"

"Your sister would still make ya go see your jerk-off nephew, anyway, Timmy."

"If you'd married Dolly, maybe you would've had a house and a pool, too, Artie."

"I was too good of a guy. Dolly hadda have a loser like Jimmy—she needed a project. Little Jimmy was her project."

Tim pointed to the checkerboard, wiping his forehead and neck again. "Artie, you can't make that move."

"Bullshit, I'm retired. I can make any damn move I want. I don't have ta listen ta any two-bit night club owner—or wait for a call from any cheapskate 'twofer' promoter, anymore."

"Wait for a call? You never had a damn phone. Maybe you didn't hear the pay phone jangling from down the hall."

"How could I with the ringing in my ears from you pounding on your damn organ."

"Piano—"

"Whatever…"

Tim replaced Arthur's checker in its original position and made another move. "Maybe you heard, but you never listened, Artie. Same as Gabby Martini never listened when I told him to stop boozing and smoking so much. I could've gotten a better response with talking to the wall. You heard about 'High Ball' Martini, didn't you, you heard, right?"

"Heard? Heard what?"

"Gabby Martini's third wife, Rosezina, told me."

"Told ya…?"

"Gabby didn't make it through his last operation, poor devil."

"What! Why didn't ya call me, Timmy. Christ, ya shoulda told me straight out!"

"Rosezina called, saying that she saw it in the *Hoboken News*. I felt a tightness, the minute she told me."

"He was in Jersey?"

"Page 13—Deaths Elsewhere. She said she knew we'd want to know."

"Such a damn star." Arthur made several gyrations from the waist up with his arms and shoulders, as if he were doing a soft shoe dance.

"One of the best, of the best." Tim unbuttoned his shirt collar.

"Jeezus, that's two—wonder who'll be the third one."

"What third you talking about, Artie, what third?"

"What do I mean—whatta I mean? Everybody knows that when two stars die, there's always a third. Everybody knows that. It's a fact."

"Naw, that's a crock of shit, Artie. Don't believe that stuff."

"I'm telling ya—Jimmy BelAire, Gabby 'High Ball' Martini… It's a fact, the same as you being a star is a fact."

"Me? A star? Not me, Artie, I was never a star. You were more of a star than me."

"Bullshit—of course ya was a star. Ya played the Island. Anybody who plays the Island is a bonafide star."

"Coney Island? You played Coney Island yourself, Artie. You almost played Atlantic City."

"Not Coney Island, for chrissake, not Coney Island. Santa Catalina—the ballroom—the Avalon ballroom."

"I never played Santa Catalina, Artie."

"Sure ya did, technically."

"I remember getting the call to go out there once, in case The Great Calypso cancelled. He was a hell of a pill popper. Said it was because of the war…"

"But, ya see—you was there! It was a done deal. You'd rehearsed and was ready ta go. If the Great Calypso had caved in, you was ready to step right in. Ya had it nailed and woulda been the warm-up act before the show came on. Your move." Arthur resumed the dance movement with his upper body.

"Besides I never even got out to the damn island. I got to the pier and they said Cappy Calypso had already taken the boat across with the other guys. I waited at that little calamari restaurant for hours before going home. It was the beginning of the end for me. Cecilia and I started drifting apart after that—forty years ago this month."

"Forty? This month—Jeezus…" Arthur drew his hand down over his mouth and chin.

"My ambition went south to Yucatán or somewhere."

"You and CeCe was like water and oil. Didn't I always tell ya that? You two never woulda made it together anyway."

"No, we could've made it if people—some of my so-called buddies—didn't keep sticking their noses in our business. Thinking they knew what was best for us. Maybe we should have kicked everybody out of our life, then our marriage might have worked out different."

"Naw, it's a fact that once the candle goes out it's over. Ya can't restart it."

"You mean relight it." Tim palmed two of Arthur's checkers.

"Whatever… Anyway, ya played bigger bills." Arthur scratched his chin.

"That doesn't make me a star. After awhile you and CeCe hooked up yourselves. I remember that. And I don't want to talk about it. My nephew, the doctor, says I shouldn't be upset. It's not good for my condition. Jeez it's so damn hot. You hot?"

"No. I was never a star—but you, Timmy 'Tom Tom' Thornten, was a star, I'm telling ya. I only played the North Shore. You were the bastard that we all looked up ta." Arthur removed three of Tim's checkers from the board.

"When in the hell did you ever look up to me? When did you ever say, 'break a leg', to me? You always blathered it around to everybody that I was a second fiddle."

"Second fiddle? Second fiddle, schmiddle. Timmy, I used ta tell ya that so you wouldn't get the big head is all. Ya was the type ta get the big head in those days. Ya get the big head and it messes with your concentration. In our biz, ya hadda concentrate—playing so many clubs like you did, plinkin' on the ivories. Me, I was just a hoofer, a nobody."

"For a nobody, you sure as hell found fault with everybody. Me, the big head? You got it bassackwards. You're the one that always could do no wrong. You blamed me when you thought you got dealt a lousy hand, when the timing wasn't right, or you were convinced of being in the wrong place at the wrong time. Who the hell was full of himself?"

"Not me. I remember being booked for Valentine's Day weekend at Bill and Pauline's Big Rock Resort—the Catfish Room, no less." Arthur laughed and slapped his knee.

"You played the Musky Lounge, once, don't forget!"

"Don't get your shorts in a bunch; remember your nephew."

"I'm not bunched. I only just have this tightness, here." Tim clutched his left side, jumped two of Arthur's pieces and swept them off the board.

"So what is this, I ask ya—checkmate?" Arthur pointed at the checkerboard.

"We're playing checkers, you dimmy. There is no checkmate."

"There could be checkmate, is all I'm saying. The rules, they could be amended some. I'm retired, I can do what I want—no more mister fancy-lounge owners givin' the thumbs down, no more sonofabitch big-shot promoters not spendin' a dime ta call. I never had it good like dinky Jimmy BelAire, 'High Ball' Martini, and you. It was always a struggle for me, living outta old cars, on the road constantly, stayin' overnight in roach motels. My type a gig was the bottom rung is what the hell I'm sayin'—whale poop."

"You think I had it easy? I had to take the bus a lot of times to make my gigs. I was in the next room to you at those roach motels. Then I had to have the clubs tune their lousy pianos before anything came out right."

"You refuse to believe reality, Timmy. I don't know what for. Maybe it makes ya feel better, hurtin' me like this. I don't know…"

"Let me tell you something about hurting, 'Dancing' Donamann. Let me tell you about the pain when you and CeCe shacked up together in that little flat you rented in Rockaway. Me, kicked out—" Tim clutched at his chest, slumped over, and knocked some checkers off the table as he sank to the ground.

A jogger veered off the park path and rushed up to the table. "What's happened? Can I help?"

"Naw—he's Tim 'Tom Tom' Thornten, one of the best acts, ta this day."

The jogger bent down. "Don't think he's acting today, man. Hey, Tom can you hear me?"

"Tim—his name's, Tim." Arthur said.

"Do you have a cell phone? We'd better call 911!"

Arthur moved to Tim's side and leaned close to him. "Ha—he's just fainted or somethin' from the heat's all."

"Better get help, could be serious," the jogger said, turning away and scanning the park for more assistance.

"Timmy, Timmy. Listen. I'm sorry, I'm sorry," Arthur said. "I never meant it ta be like this. It was all just a little fun with ya, here. I was just playin' ya is all. Come on now. CeCe never went for me like she did you. It was just a fling, me 'n her. I was always just a tomcat. Ya know that. I couldn't confess to being up to my old tricks—I had no guts, no ahla ahla's. Then after awhile it didn't seem ta matter, when she threw me out. Why say somethin' then? You two was back together and gettin' along swell again. There seemed no need ta say anything. Now get up, will ya?"

Tim nodded as his eyes glazed over.

"I was the one who sent the booking telegram for the Avalon that night so you'd be outta the picture for a while, so I could schmooze CeCe. I knew that Cappy's agent hadda back-up act in case he popped one too many. I didn't see it comin' that you and CeCe would break up over such a little thing like that. Didn't know you two's marriage was so dicey, I swear. Timmy, buddy—stars don't always go in threes. Not always. Everybody knows that. It's a fact…"

Popular Mechanics

In the sunrise of his youth, the boy's mother, Yelena, often remarked that he was like a fragile little bird: thin of bone, thin of frame, thin of gait. She didn't hold much trust that he would be able to lead an empowered life.

His father kept to himself, paying scant attention to his son and everyone else as well. This father, Wenzel Soaring, often stared off into the distance as though he saw something that the rest of them couldn't quite catch.

It was said that Wenzel had flown in one day on the heels of World War II, when all over the world there were mass displacements of people. He had swept Yelena off her feet and settled into small-town domestic life. No one knew where he had come from or anything about him.

The parents named their son Travis, soon changed to Henry, because Yelena had a large and extended family spread across the township, all with too many T's and V's sprinkling their names: Rivten, Trevin, Verton, and the like. People presumed that Wenzel probably had one or two distant relatives somewhere.

"That name, Travis, didn't seem to fit the boy," was all his father said when asked.

Henry didn't think "Henry" suited him either, so when one of his uncles called him Hal one day, he clutched on to it like a sparrow's foot around a telephone wire and never again answered to anything else.

Hal's youth was spent in the small, flat, Midwestern town of Belvidere Park—the county seat, where the farmers gathered on Saturdays. Some condescending visitors referred to the burg as being misspelled.

Very early one summer morning little Hal heard a Katydid thrumming. Its siren song pulled him out into the neighborhood. Hal hiked down the street to his cousin's house. Reaching up, he opened the latch on the tall backyard gate. Inside he saw a swing set with a plastic pony hitched by four large springs. Excitement overcame him. He wanted to ride the wild-eyed creature. He saddled up and before he knew it the beast had thrown him—a real dustup. Something pulled, something cracked, and something hurt. He was on his back with a cloud roiling over him. Through his tears he saw his two small cousins, noses pressed against the glass, staring out of the kitchen window at him. They didn't move. Hal's aunt stood behind them in shadow. Both youngsters looked up over their shoulders at their mother as she drew the window curtains closed, hiding them from his view.

Shaken, Hal stood up after a few minutes and wobbled home to his mother. Yelena, absorbed in singing Yma Sumac's *Lure of the Unknown Love*, was oblivious to what had happened to her son as he came into their backyard where she was pinning up laundry to dry on the clothes line.

* * *

Hal took to wearing a jacket and became a horizontal boy after the accident in his cousins' yard. He stayed flat, level, close to the ground and shunned the upright, perpendicular of a vertical boy. He felt shaky on his tricycle, would not climb trees or fences, couldn't be made to pick cherries for his father, and had a difficult time getting winter clothes down from the closet shelf for his mother. His parents labeled it his "Untowards."

Yelena, talking with relatives at parties and picnics, replied that Hal was having an uneventful childhood outside of a certain posture and disposition to slouch. She couldn't recall anything catastrophic, disastrous, or devastating happening to the boy. The family nodded their heads in understanding, and gave Hal sidelong glances, intent that he might not see what they saw in him.

"Look, there," one of Yelena's brothers said. "See the way he does that?"

"You mean the hunching," a sister remarked.

"And the walk, watch his walk."

Early in school, when he should have been paying more attention to his teachers, Hal developed a habit of staring off in reverie like his father. Even so, he not only proved to be an average student, but he also proved his mother wrong about his being fragile, by fighting when others called him "buzzard-back," "crick-back," or "Quasimodo-back." His earliest adversaries were his cousins, then neighborhood children and, later, schoolmates. He flaunted only a few bruises, smashed knuckles, and swollen eyes for his pride of flying in the face of derision.

In grade school, his father's attention was tweaked, when Hal liberated the old man's tools and his cherished *Popular Mechanics* magazines. In high school, Hal would sneak the family car for midnight runs. Some tools found their way back. The car, worse for wear always returned. However, the magazines seldom, if ever, were brought back.

Hal cultivated an innate affinity for the mysterious workings and goings on of gears, springs, ratchets, and odd-shaped little pieces that settled into the dark cores and crevices of engines, no matter what type. The *Popular Mechanics* magazines became his best friends, opening his eyes to more esoteric reading materials from the old Carnegie Library. He left his fighting behind. In his dreams, he traced looping wires and fuel lines, electrical circuits, and compound hinges. However, one nightmare remained vivid, wherein Leonardo de Vinci's drawings of winged flying machines swirled through his night vision, their mechanisms undulating, undulating, undulating. When the wings began to melt, Hal would jerk awake, with a taste of stinging sour bile in his throat which he took to be the taste of fear.

Sometime during Youth's High Noon, he became friends with Keith Cleery when they were both scraping bottom for friends and drawn to the acrid smell of the methanol and oil mixture used for model airplane fuel.

Their respective fathers took their sons to the city park. Keith's father sat in his car reading pulp fiction while Keith, somewhat portly with brown hair, made a nuisance of himself among the model aviators. Hal's father, on the other hand, lay stretched out the best that he could in his canvas deck chair, letting a tattered edition of Franz Kafka's *Metamorphosis* slip to the grass. He'd stare up at the sky in a trance as the tiny planes, tethered on thin wires, spun in circles above his head. Hal, narrow as a slide-rule, and with the promise of a dark uni-brow, hunkered close to the ground keeping his attention on the fabric and balsa wood machines vibrating from the stammering engines.

The two boys approached the eve of high school graduation, overheard nattering about the President's Volunteers in Service to America program, and decided maybe VISTA could show them a path out of their life-so-small. Hal was enthusiastic to leave right away. He then reconsidered and thought better of it. Maybe he would stay at home after all. No, in the end, knowing that he and Keith would be doing the service together, he accepted the challenge. To the awe of his family and to the astonishment of the town folk, the boys signed up for a year of service and were whisked a thousand miles down to South Carolina.

The bus arrived in the prickly heat. The passengers stepped down from the Greyhound and milled around as the driver pulled their belongings out of the cargo bay, Hal being the only one standing on the sizzling tarmac wearing his usual jacket.

* * *

The two boys worked in the back room of the VISTA Collection Center where donations were repaired and refurbished. Keith acted as a runner and office jack-of-all-trades for the news bulletin. Hal ensconced himself in a quiet corner and fixed everything that came through the door.

One year and one day later found Hal and Keith spinning in circles, trying to get a grasp on what was next after VISTA. Cicadas droned. The day was hot. The day was muggy. The day was the day that the lumber mill had a Help Wanted sign fluttering on the cyclone fence. The following morning the two of them walked into the employment office. The next day Keith settled into the Maintenance Department, and Hal was strapped onto a forklift in the warehouse because of his "Untowards." Keith climbed, while Hal stuck close to the ground. The Southerners dubbed them "Hi" and "Lo."

The two lads settled into a routine—a Dixie way of life. They boarded at Miss Winnie's Rooming House on South Street. They ate their meals at Dean's Café where the counter was their schooling—their daily lessons. They listened to the chatter of the locals echoing around the room, overheard that everybody knew everyone else's business, and that most families were related in some way: kin, marriage, or divorce. Better not say anything about a woman you see because her husband, brother, or father might be sitting next to you. More importantly, they learned that any family having somebody working at a steady job and bringing home a paycheck would immediately be moved up a few rungs to the middle class on the social ladder, without having to pass Go.

In August, during one of the hottest days of the summer's hot-spells, over chocolate malts outside the ice cream parlor, Hal and Keith met Savanna Murfes and her best friend, Lizzette Twang. As soon as Hal saw Savanna he got the squirmies, the clammy hands, the foggy head. Keith stuttered, although he never had before. He got the Him-Haws; and, if asked, he couldn't explain how to put one foot in front of the other to Lizzette.

Whenever the question arose, Savanna said that she came by her name because Daddy's car broke down twenty miles from town and she was delivered under the lube rack at a gas station in Georgia instead of in the hospital in South Carolina. She always felt some guilt about it. Not the lube rack, she was quick to correct, but the fact that it happened in Georgia. Lizzette was proud never to have been west of Longnose Creek or east of Barton Slough.

Savanna and Lizzette could tell that clearly, connections were being made. Savanna saw a bright light descend around her. Her hand itched. Later, she folded and rubbed her arms to ward off the shivers. Later, Savanna's brothers, Arvell and Bubba Murfes, knew as they sprawled on the davenport of their mama's house. Even later, Savanna's Papa knew as he argued a bad back instead of work. Then Mama did something so rare that everyone in the Murfes' household who was sitting around the supper table looked at each other in amazement—she cracked a wisp of a smile.

A few blocks away, Lizzette knew so well that she dumped her boyfriend, Cody, out of the front porch swing and kicked him off the property saying she needed more room—he was stifling her. She couldn't take a cigarette out of a pack without him there to light a match for her, like she couldn't do that for herself. She confided in Savanna that she was ready to see a new face around anyway because she'd seen Cody's red hair and freckles since his family moved into town during the second grade.

Arvell and Bubba sat outside Krenshaw's Hardware whittling and smiling. They also smiled as they loitered just outside of the side gate at the mill waiting with their sister as Hal walked out to the parking lot on payday. At home they smiled as they called, "Ma! Need some more beers, here!" and kept an eye on the thin young man with the fat wallet.

Savanna's Papa got his septic pump fixed, courtesy of Hal's magic with mechanics. Arvell and Bubba began dreaming again of hidden gas tanks, white lighting, and new-moon nights. The family never confided to any other relative, neighbor, or town folk that they nodded to, about their hidden treasure, the young man with the magic touch for apparatus that believed in the sun rising and setting on their sweet Savanna's derriere. They were on the step up into genteel society and if others were left behind, so be it.

There came a time in spring when Savanna implored Hal to move out of Miss Winnie's Rooming House and into the back porch of the old Murfes homestead, across the river from the mill, where generations of the Murfes clan had been conceived and laid out. There was the musty day bed, the ratty old foot locker, and a clothesline strung on two nails over the rusted washtub. It was out of the way, a remote little nest different from the way the rest of the family lived. Savanna held up three finely manicured fingers, ticking off the good points. The street was shady, the dogs lazy, and high water never reached the stoop. Hal considered all the negatives: the brothers, Papa and Mama, and the smell of the lumber mill. In the end there was no escape when Savanna, poured into her short cut-offs, paraded before him in her tight cotton t-shirt and fondled her strawberry-blonde hair. Hal had no defense for the maneuvers she was capable of.

Savanna's mother took a keen interest in Hal's health after he brought her washing machine back from the Hereafter. She made sure he got the best cut of meat, extra helpings of grits, and a refresh on his coffee. At that juncture, Arvell and Bubba searched everywhere, but couldn't find a smile to stick on their faces.

* * *

On a sultry, autumn evening with a full moon above and Savanna's abundance below, Hal fell into delirium and asked Savanna to marry him.

For her part, the young belle clamped down on the young man's proposal like she was pulling a channel cat out of fast-moving river water rushing over a sandbar. The wedding was planned for the following spring. Other plans were formed by Lizzette and Keith, with their wedding set for the first of April. Lizzette defended the timing with age-old logic that Savanna couldn't be maid-of-honor and a bride on the same day, so somebody had to get married first. Besides, the weather would be nicer later on in May or June for her best friend and Hal.

Hi and Lo were now deep into a Dixie way of life. They knew that, soon as the vows were taken, they should take their new wives home to Belvidere Park where corn was king. However, their brides-to-be were happy already at home. So were their families, content with the fact that everything should remain undisturbed; they wouldn't abide Yankee fire-brand talk about journeys, farewells, and such.

Arvell and Bubba saw no need for Hal to purchase his own car for they had resurrected their 1940 Ford coupe along with his help. It rattled, it shook, and the ground was framed through the rusted-out floorboards. The brothers said times were great. Savanna said times were even better than that.

Her Papa relaxed his back and asked Hal for an advance to see him through the week. He thought like a Politician, a Big Shot. "A little fa-vor—boy," he'd say with a hand out and a broad toothy grin. Savanna nodded her approval with a tender smile and open purse. Hal winced with a sigh and pulled out his wallet.

"Put it on my tab—boy," old-man Murfes would say sliding away from the counter at Dean's Cafe.

Mama began dreaming of a grandchild as the weather turned cooler—a grandchild that would be the new generation beer-runner for her boys. When no one was looking she smiled to herself, humming "Look Away Dixie Land."

* * *

Hal and Keith were drinking coffee one day and Keith touched on the subject of going back to the Midwest. He said that he was fed up with

43

Cody's practical jokes which began after he and Lizzette had started dating.

The first dirty trick occurred when Hal and Keith were on their lunch break and Keith was distracted. Cody switched Keith's coffee cup with a cup of hot gravy. When Keith gagged and spit it out everybody else around the table had a good laugh. The jokes moved on to Cody switching Keith's cigarettes with candy cigarettes. Another good laugh followed with everyone calling him "little wuss" when he opened them and shook one out.

One morning Cody brought in an old cardboard box full of his Great Grand- Daddy's Confederate War trophies. He said he was ready to trade or sell. During the morning he hid them under Keith's bench. Before noon he claimed that his family's things had been stolen and headed up a search.

Luckily, Hal asked Keith for a wrench to fix the forklift. Keith said he had a wrench somewhere on his bench, and to go and get it. Hal discovered the cardboard box and moved it under a nearby table. The Northern boys knew that they had dodged a bullet when the Civil War heirlooms weren't found in Keith's possession. The game was on. It was turning into cat and mouse, of bob and weave, of x's and o's.

The following day, Keith said to Hal, "My driver's license is up for renewal back home. Keep it under your hat. I'm just popping up North for a quick visit. Be back before you're able to saw grass or see weed."

"Get one here," Hal said. "You can use it anywhere, back in the Midwest as well. Lizzette'll be proud of your mastery of southern driving. Use it when you take her North."

"Don't think that's in the Lizzette family mix. Some of them already have a keen interest in my license, as though they'd like to get their hands on it. Misplace it, lose it, maybe. It's a muckin' fess all right." Keith slumped back.

Hal said, "Yup, the Murfes brothers always seem to be like two mangy hyenas lurking just out of reach of a lion with its prey. Always prowling, waiting for an opening to duck in for a piece of the carcass. Can't do any work themselves, but they'll take all the scraps they can stuff into their bellies."

"At least the Twangs only have Junior for that and he can't be as bad as the two of them," Keith said.

Living circumstances began to percolate in Hal's mind. Facts began to add up. Savanna's family meeting him at the gate after work, sitting a few rows away at the movies, Mama hovering in the stores, and Papa waiting outside the bank on payday flashed through his mind. In addition, Savanna making out the bills, giving him a little cash for the week, saying the rest is for my Hope Chest. It's for the dowry. It's for us. Keith admitted to the same on his side of the fence.

Soon, Hi and Lo put their heads together and began to talk about Dixie life. Soon, Hal and Keith had company join them for lunch on the loading dock. Lizzette's Uncle Ferrell got all chummy. Cody, Lizzette's spurned boyfriend, and second cousin on the Murfes side of the family, settled in close, next to the truck scale. A knot began to wrap around Hal's gut.

End-of-the-year holidays were peeking over the horizon. Hi and Lo formulated a plan. They cut back on incidentals, kept their eyes glued to the ground for money, and scrounged for loose change anywhere they could think of: furniture, car seats, vending machines, and telephone booths. Whatever could help them out for their getaway.

All Souls Day found the two of them going over their meager haul. It wasn't looking good. Hal sat down between two stacks of pallets to think about it as Keith went back to work. The rich smell of the pine resin surrounded him. He was staring at the railroad tracks when he saw Cody push a wheelbarrow out and dump a load of shingles off the dock. In a few minutes, Ferrell backed a company truck alongside the building, scooped the shingles into the bed, and drove toward the rear of the property.

The following day Hal and Keith hid and watched Cody and Ferrell repeat the exchange. After they returned to work, Hal followed the same chickweed path to the back of the property that Ferrell had taken. A pile of wood rested next to an opening in the galvanized fencing. The next day, Hal discovered a load of shingles culled from the warehouse inventory hidden under an old tarp next to the loading dock. It was time to roll the dice. He spray-painted the shingles' edges.

Sitting in the front room before supper on Friday night at the Murfes homestead, Hal stared at the ceiling. "I saw Ferrell at lunch; looked as though he missed a nail and banged a finger. It seemed to be troubling him."

"Oh, he ain't fretful 'bout the finger. He's worried if he'll get his house roofed 'fore the rains come is all." Arvell winked.

Papa slouched back in his chair. "Wahl, he's got Cody helpin'."

"They're a team all right," Hal said.

"They'll finish by the weekend. Whole damn family's pourin' over his roof like a bunch of beans on pork," old-man Murfes said.

On Monday morning, Hal said to Keith, "We need a car." They sat in silence for a few minutes.

With his tongue, Keith rolled a match stick around in his mouth and leaned forward. "Where do you do it?"

"Where do I do what?"

"You and Savanna. Where do you bang her? Lizzette and I do it back of the house. In the garage."

"Oh," Hal said.

"It's the only place that we can sneak off to without getting caught."

"You're just kidding yourselves if you don't think Lizzette's mother hasn't got eyes on you two," Hal said.

"Think so?"

"Yup—"

Keith said, "Reason I mention it. There's an old '54 Buick buried in that shed under a pile of junk. That's what we use—the back seat."

Hal sat up straight. "Maybe I can get over there to take a look at it."

It was all very Southern Polite, Hal and Keith called Ferrell and Cody to join them in the back of the warehouse. Uncle Ferrell could finish his roofing job with the mill's shingles if the "beans" hadn't gotten the job squared away yet. The spray paint that Hal had used on the wood would remain hidden so there would be no need to tear the painted shingles off the house. The only thing that had to be reported back to the two families was—nothing. It was all set, Hal would help out Lizzette's family, nothing to report, sir. Heads nodded in agreement.

"Oh, and I need a little money for some car parts, too." Hal said.

Ferrell frowned, "You got no car."

"Lizzette's family needs to get one going is all," Hal smiled.

"Bullshit—" Cody curled his upper lip.

Ferrell cut him off. "Can't have no buckets sittin' around inside of a house all winter."

"Suppose not." Cody scuffed the floor with his boot.

A day later, Hal and Keith stood in the back yard waiting for Lizzette's mother to unlock the front doors of the sagging garage.

Keith spoke low and held his hand in front of his mouth. "It's been in there ever since Lizzette's old man got killed."

Hal said, "How'd it happen?"

"Her mother, Jacinda, says he was killed by a New England Presbyterian minister. She's never forgiven him."

"Oh?" Hal said.

"Yeah, her father threw a scythe at a truck that came close to clipping him when he was working off a DUI on a road gang. The truck braked, the minister was following the truck and lost control of his car, hitting her dad."

They moved into the dusty half-light of the garage and pried up the hood of the car. Everyone gathered around as Hal studied the engine.

"What we have here is a mess up with the Fornortner Rod. It's hitting the Sadapo Ring on the bi-angus," he said, examining the engine cavity of the old white Buick. Lizzette's mother and stepfather, Sherman, nodded their heads as though they understood. Junior, on the other side of the cowling, mimed a "yeah" in agreement.

Hal looked at him. "You see?" Junior passed a funny little sound that could be mistaken for a sigh.

"I can see how it might be," Keith said with a grin, hunching over the toothy looking grill.

Savanna and Lizzette sat on the back porch glider playing at wedding plans, glancing toward the garage now and then. The two Pollyannas were proud that their men were about to get the car running, contemplating cruising through town with their girlfriends' envious eyes on them.

"It might be fixable, but that'll come later. Now, we have to get the garage doors all the way open and the driveway cleared in case we have to pull it out on the street for a push," Hal said.

"Count me out," Junior protested. "I got a bum knee. Can't be doin' that."

"Yeah, he's a rehabin' it on the foot rail over at Hickory Bill's Tavern." Sherman pulled his hand down over his jaw.

Junior held his hand low where Sherman couldn't see it and extended his middle finger before ambling away from the garage.

His mother, walking ahead of her son toward the house called back, "Sherm, help clean up the garage since we agreed that car had to be got rid of..."

"Jacinda, there, oughta talk to that boy of hers 'stead of me," Sherman said to no one in particular. "You know why he's down there at the tavern? Lookin' for more trouble than he'll know what to do with is what."

"How's that?" Keith said.

"He was hangin' around a time ago and this truck driver come in. Said he'd hauled some big carnie whatchamacallit up from down in Florida winter quarters. A piece of junk he called it—put him in a bad mood. Had to pack it uphill and help old man Carpus, over yonder, set it up after un-loadin': wet, cold, dirty work. Him and Jun got into it—probably from Junior drinkin' too much and not thinkin' too much. Driver put him down, messed up his knee. Now the kid hangs out down there cuddlin' a tire iron hopin' the guy'll be back in so he can even the score. . ."

Even with hearing Jacinda Twang's orders, Sherman steered clear of the garage, and Junior resumed his watch at the tavern, leaving Hal and Keith free to work on the car.

Two days later, Hal said that the Buick was ready to go. All Keith had to do was gas it up without the Twangs' knowledge. He would meet Keith downtown after work.

With preparations in place, they kept to their daily routines. That night, Savanna's father excused himself from the supper table, saying he needed to put together some Carolina rigs with Sherman before they went cat fishing the next day.

Mother Murfes said, "I wish Papa would be a little careful there with that Sherman. Anybody'd name a son Sherman hereabouts gotta have a screw loose or somethin'. At least it's better than when Lizzette hung out with our Cody. I worried about Sherman being kin when that happened."

Savanna said, "Oh, Mama, Papa knows enough about runnin' set lines for cat fishin'. He just takes Sherm along to help, 'cause of his back."

"Speaking of which," Hal said, "I think I might have pulled a muscle in my back at work, so I'm turning in early."

He exaggerated his gait and hobbled toward the back porch. He gathered his essentials and lay in bed too nervous to fall asleep. He had just dropped off when he woke with a start, thinking he was still in the middle of a bad dream. He realized, awake, that he was *living* in the middle of a nightmare.

All day at the mill Hal went through the motions of work, waiting for the afternoon whistle to blow. He mused that it must be like the stories his uncle had told him of the war, hours of boredom broken by moments of terror.

* * *

Arvell and Bubba joined Hal as he left work, falling into step with him until they reached Dean's Café where they always parked the car. They sat down on the worn bench outside the diner and wedged Hal between them. Suddenly Keith swung the Buick around the corner. Three sets of eyes followed the path of the large, white vehicle as, according to plan, it slowed to pick up Hal, sped up, and headed west out of town. Hal could do nothing. At least it looked as if Keith would be able to get away and make it across the state line.

When the two brothers brought Hal through the front door of the Murfes' house, pandemonium had broken out. Word had already spread, snapping over the telephone lines, that Lizzette's Keith was missing with the car. Questions were raised, accusations were made, fingers were pointed, and they were all directed at Hal.

"What the hell's goin' on?"

"How'd he get the car?"

"I've got to get over to Lizzette's!"

"Arvell, take your sister."

"Where'd he go?"

"What the hell's goin' on?"

"Shee-it!"

"Somebody's payin' the ole Piper Man for this one! Lettin' that damn Yankee, Keith, get off his chain."

Hal had no driver's license, little of his own money, and only the ware-house mule to drive. He played dumb as to Keith's plans. The Murfes family had him in their crosshairs though with the disappearance of his buddy.

The following morning he picked up his lunch pail, and eased the screen door shut behind him as Savanna slept upstairs. Reaching the sidewalk, Arvell fell into step behind him.

Hal turned to the older brother, "Morning, hanging around like ugly wallpaper, I see."

Arvell's face twisted into something between a grimace and a crooked smile. Bubba pulled up beside them in the coupe, reaching over and opening the passenger side door. Hal was guided into the back seat. Arvell climbed in, and they headed toward the mill.

In the afternoon, Hal swung the forklift under a pallet of concrete blocks, drove out through the back fence where the shingles had flown and down the dirt path. Double puffs of dust, kicked up from the small hard tires, rose like miniature contrails following him off the property and around the corner.

The '40 Ford was parked in its usual spot. He pulled up behind the car and lowered the full pallet against the rear bumper. He took out a box cutter and sunk the blade into both rear tires. The car heaved a sigh and slumped as stale, rubber-laden air rushed over his hand.

Hal drove the forklift up the street toward the bus station. Coming to the intersection at First Street, he caught sight of Cody's rundown dark-blue Plymouth. Parking the mule, he reached in through the driver's side window and opened the door. A moment later, he had the car hot-wired and was pulling away from the curb as Cody emerged from Shan's Tavern with a six-pack of Dixie Beer under his arm. Hal waved goodbye through the rear window and headed west toward the county highway.

Shadows moved over the asphalt as Hal tried to pick the turnoff that he thought would take him the quickest to the state line. The two-lane road looped around the hills and through the trees. Thirty minutes from town he thought that his direction might be wrong; thirty-five minutes from town he met a car coming toward him. The driver waved. Hal glanced into the rearview mirror. Brake lights blinked before the vehicle moved on.

Forty minutes brought him around a sharp curve. Tire marks charred the pavement ahead and swung wildly from side-to-side before disappearing through a guardrail.

Hal hit the brakes.

A tow truck blocked the road. It angled down the embankment. With a slow gait, a rotund Sheriff's deputy walked over to the Plymouth. He ducked his head, staring into the car. His mirror sunglasses seemed to reflect all of the South. "Jest be a minute," he said. "They're pulling a wreck outta the crick."

Hal stared through the windshield. A barrel of a man wearing greasy dark blue overalls pushed one of the levers on the back of the truck. A great mangled white carcass moved into view, crawling inexorably toward the truck.

A searing metallic sensation rose in Hal's throat as though he had a mouthful of liquid nails. The Buick settled into place behind the truck.

"Fatality. Coroner just hauled him off," the deputy said, looking over his shoulder.

The truck driver pulled himself up into the cab of the truck. Diesel belched from the stack as the tow truck moved past the Plymouth. The Deputy jerked his arm and waved Hal forward.

Wanting to duck any questions the officer might ask, Hal grabbed the steering wheel with white knuckles and sped away. Tree limbs stretched across the narrow roadway as the broken center line jerked from side to side. Bright sunlight flashed through shadows metamorphosing into a strobe light across the asphalt ahead. Fear and loathing gripped him.

A rusted mailbox cantilevered toward the road like a hitchhiker—its raised red flag—a flashing beacon to him. A rutted farm lane snaked away up a hill and into the woods. Hal yanked the steering wheel, downshifted, and settled into the worn path. The strong smell of dank vegetation filled the car. Leafy branches slapped against the windshield as the lane climbed uphill. In a moment, he brought the Plymouth huffing into a small farmyard.

A gray-haired woman, dressed in a long tan skirt, flannel coat, and rubber boots carried an armful of firewood toward the house. She watched with narrowed eyes as the car came to a stop. Nothing moved.

Hal opened the door and eased out of the driver's seat. The woman twitched her free hand and a huge ragged hound loped down from the porch and settled in front of her. Hal greeted the pair with a big smile and apology for his unannounced arrival.

Could he get directions to the nearest bridge? He was on his way to Georgia and was mixed up direction-wise. Did she have a little gas? He was running a bit low, and there didn't seem to be any stations around. He pulled out the largest bill he had and offered it to her.

There was something needing fixing and for the money in his hand she might find a bit of gas, but only if he could look at The Something. Hal caught a movement in the shadow of the porch. A thin fellow with child-like demeanor sat in a faded rocking chair. He wore gray wool pants hitched high to the ribs, suspenders ran over angular shoulders, and once-white socks pulled taut on pale shins. He smiled with a gaping mouth that had no teeth and grasped clothes line ropes that were tied to a child's wooden horse in front of him. His body slowly moved back and forth.

"My Jimmy, there, likes 'ta ride almost better'n anything," the old woman said, following Hal's stare.

She motioned toward a looming mass, covered with canvas tarps, silhouetted against the beryline sky. Hal followed the woman as she let the firewood fall to the ground. The old cur sniffed Hal's pant leg as they approached the large round structure.

She pulled on the tarps. A slow avalanche of material slid to the ground, piling itself up in an uneven heap. At the center, a carousel stood gleaming in the lowering afternoon light.

"My Mister got it for our boy, Jimmy. Now Mister's gone'n died and it won't work."

Hal moved closer. He walked around the carnival ride. He stopped short, took a step back, sweat soaking his shirt. The carousel was perched within a few feet of a hillside.

Ground fell off abruptly behind the merry-go-round, giving a panoramic view of Tugaloo River and the valley below. The river was running dark in shadow. Bits of light broke through here and there where the timber was sparse while the taller trees along its shore still caught the sunlight.

Hal saw that the old woman's husband must have been in the middle of repairing the carousel's motor. Hal knelt down to examine it. Remnants of motor parts and tools lay scattered near the hoofs of the horses. He raised his eyes, taking in bright colors of the mounts and their bridles. Sharp contours of legs flowed into the straining backs and necks. The heads, canted and thrown at wild angles, glared at him with eyes bulged and nostrils flared.

With shaking hands he set to work. Twenty minutes later he was replacing the motor's housing after repairing the open circuit in the field coil of the commutator. He oiled and greased the last pieces, tightened up the bolts, and plugged the motor's electrical cord into the socket. The engine sprang to life. Hal ratcheted it into gear and the merry-go-round began to turn.

The old woman let out a yelp and slapped her knee. "Wahl I'll be dog!" Tar Shack Granny said so, Tar Shack Granny said so," she chanted. "I know'd it. Soon as I seen that white of your'n car I know'd what she said was trueful."

"But the car's dark blue." Hal said, swinging off the ride.

The old woman pointed to the bumper and right front fender. "There," she said.

Hal saw a wide streak of white paint. Then its import swept over him.

"Old Granny living in da shack down yonder, she tol' me a angel'd come and make it right for my Mister and my Jimmy. And angels is always covered in white and all."

A burp, burp, burp sound came from the direction of the driveway. Ferrell's diesel truck swung through the trees followed by Arvell and Bubba's '40 Ford. Before the meager dust settled, four men emerged from the vehicles. Cody paused to glance into the Plymouth as they advanced. He slipped a book of matches out of his shirt pocket and tossed it onto the car's dashboard.

Horizontal Hal studied the men. Horizontal Hal stared at the carousel that teetered on the edge of the precipice and gathered his strength.

Something deep in his core told Hal to jump. He sprang onto the gyrating platform. Tremors shot through him. He reached the motor and threw it into high gear. The carousel picked up speed. Hal felt the pull and whip of the whirling floor. He staggered between the pumping horses. Their wild eyes and gleaming teeth threw him back to his cousin's yard, crashing into the hard dirt, and the rocking horse's fierce glower. He was nauseous.

Arvell and Bubba tried to grip the thin steel poles as the carousel flew past them. Ferrell picked Cody up by his shirt collar with one hand and britches with the other, pitching him onto the gyrating merry-go-round. The young man slammed into one seat and bounced around several ponies. Stunned, he tried to keep from sliding off, attempted to protect his head, and struggled to get his bearings. The three other men urged him to go after Hal.

Arvell shouted, "Turn off the motor!"

Bubba roared, "Cody! There he is! There he is!" Cody, dazed, glanced around, rubbing his head.

Hal scrambled onto the back of a seat and gripped the cornice trim, trying to access the roof. He felt a grip on his coat, then a tug as it was ripped off with a splitting of the seams. The carousel's rotation increased as the motor whined out of control. Ferrell threw a piece of firewood at Hal. With a bang it ricocheted off the roof.

Centrifugal force yanked Hal's feet away from the seat. Arvell's face got in the way and the older brother staggered back from the blow to his head.

Another tear resonated as Hal's shirt caught on a sharp edge. A gigantic pull sucked him toward the top of the carousel. Finger by finger his grip loosened and he tumbled head-over-heels away from the structure.

The only sensation he felt was an eeriness of no ground beneath him and lunatic silence. A scalding feeling high up in his chest was so intense that it became his whole world.

Falling, his body responded by pushing his shoulders down and arms up, then shoulders up and arms down which drove his body higher. His peripheral vision caught great wings thrusting to keep him airborne. He glided in the upper sunlight, acclimating to the alien surroundings, banked left, then right. A vision of Savanna jumped out at him. She would be waiting for him. He felt the tug to veer toward her, swoop low, and carry her off.

The old woman's thin voice flew up to him, "Jumping Jehovah! Great God Almighty! Ah know'd it was a angel."

Hal banked left again by raising his right wing and headed toward the broad Tugaloo River. Georgia waited for him on the other side. The sun dipped behind a cloud bank far off in the West—it was beginning to set. Staring into the distance, Hal, instead, saw in it the beginning of a new day.

She Left Him for a Woman She Hid Under Her Bed

Now Abberhider Quikley is somewhat prepared if he gets any inkling of the unexpected—not as he was last year between National Boss' Day and Thanksgiving. He looks back on that time with bittersweet memories of confusion, loss, and mortification.

It was a Wednesday when Abberhider stepped through the front door of his Georgian-Colonial style home and into the quiet foyer as his two dogs, Ollie, the Bulldog, and Stan, the American Foxhound, minced in circles and whined. "Where's Cleo?" he asked them. Their eyes remained riveted on him. Ah, they were coy little scallywags weren't they, not telling tales out of school, not giving him a clue to work with. Removing his hat he instructed the dogs to sit, petted them, and hung up his coat before trying to locate his wife to ask why she had not been at the train station to pick him up.

He walked through the house calling her name. He rearranged the sofa pillows in the living room, squared a chair in the dining room, returned a book to its proper place in the library, and surveyed the kitchen. Climbing the stairs, he entered the master bedroom with the dogs padding behind him.

There on his dresser was a note:

Abb, you asinine ass,

I know you will be devastated, but I've left with the Aruban woman that I've been hiding under my bed—will call.

-Cleo

P.S.—Her name is Gosalvez, Gosalvez Anthony.

Abberhider scrutinized his wife's bold handwriting racing across the back of a Cruise Mecca itinerary in scarlet ink. The brochure was from the *For-Old-Times-Sake* holiday that Abb had taken Cleo to in the West Indies. It had been their twenty-fifth wedding anniversary and they had gone to Barbados. He turned the brochure over, staring at the unmistakable precise jabs, made by Cleo's nail file through the smiling face of Valerie Phling, their tour guide, whom they'd met in Speightstown. Abberhider ran his thumb over the corner of Valerie's eye, as though wiping away a tear.

He hurried into Cleo's bedroom and looked at the bed. It was identical to his of course, because he had bought both of them for the master suite. It was only later that Cleo had him move her bed into the guest room, saying his snoring, his tossing and turning, his squeaks and whistles were unbearable, making it impossible for her to get any real REM sleep.

He measured the bed with his eyes and wondered how Cleo could hide someone under it, and for how long—surely not more than a few hours at most. Questions swirled through his mind: had his wife merely left the house to buy cigarettes or was her absence of a more ominous nature? Why hadn't she mentioned this other woman to him? Why was the note handwritten when the laptop sat on the desk next to the window?

He tried comprehending his wife's message as he straightened one corner of the drooping bedspread. Cleo's left breast had been the same at one time, before he'd nagged her to have it lifted with an implant, which her mother referred to as her daughter having been tucked and rolled. Cleo's mother had then proceeded to tell her daughter that she hated Abberhider. Abb couldn't understand why. It wasn't as if the procedure had been done in Tijuana.

The dogs snuffled around the room as though they suddenly caught the scent of an intruder and wanted to pick up the trail. Abberhider released a sigh and turned off the light. The dogs galloped downstairs. They lifted their muzzles as if to test the air before baying. A drawn out howl echoed through the hallway. Ollie wheeled and stared up at Abb, cocking his head to one side. Stanley squatted behind the newel post and gaped through the balusters. Abberhider gathered himself together, cleared his throat, and let them out of the back door, realizing with anguish that for the first time he might have to clean up after them.

He was dozing in his recliner when the call came in. Out of habit he checked his watch before picking up the receiver.

"Hello, the Quikley residence."

"Abb—this is Cleo. I'm sorry but I had to do this—don't interrupt—even though I know you must have a million questions. The three of us can get together later, maybe this weekend, somewhere that's public, and discuss it more fully. I'm sorry but we had to take the BMW in case you haven't checked the garage. I'll call you, Saturday."

Abb said, "But what about this Arabian woman?" Cleo was gone with a stinging click of the receiver.

Their new BMW? Shit, of all things. He'd hardly had a chance to put any miles on it himself. He visualized the car getting smaller and smaller as it wound its way down the tree-lined street with the cocky little cartoon character from the dealership on the license plate holder laughing at him. He wanted to crush the pompous little troll in his fist, leaving Mister Happy Face grimacing like a toothless old curmudgeon.

Abberhider reflected on the fact that it had been almost a week since he and Cleo had spoken on the phone as he waited for her in Giorgio's new Left Bank Restaurant. Cleo, tall, L'Oreal-Preference blond, dressed in a charcoal gray Prada pants suit, with Gucci handbag, arrived with the other woman shadowing her. The other woman, a short swarthy female, with orange and purple-color hair, wore a Levi leather jacket and Gottschalks leather pants, adorned with laces and buckles, eyelets and rings, straps and cleats. When she plodded past a table one of the small metal gargoyles on her cuff snagged on a napkin, whipping it to the floor. Gosalvez was the most peculiar creature that Abb had ever seen. Her rotund body, from double chin and buffalo hump to protruding waist, was a perfect foil to her long thin arms and legs. Abberhider was enamored with her extremely long fingers. He felt giddy with an unexplained feeling of perverse euphoria and tried not to gawk at the woman.

Cleo lowered her Louis Vuitton sunglasses and waved. Watching, as she made her way toward him, a frowning Abberhider sat stiff in a window seat. She swiveled her hips around adjacent tables, ever the new age matador teasing the staid mixed-modern chairs. "Orange and Purple Hair" took up a strategic position at a nearby table, facing him a few feet away. Abb saw her small clutch disappear and became uneasy, picturing the muzzle of a Beretta—maybe a silver one, no, with her it would be a black piece—creep up over the edge of the white linen tablecloth. He made sure that his wife sat between them. If the other one was going to take a shot at him she would have to work for it.

Cleo made herself comfortable and ordered her usual glass of Bonneau du Martray Chardonnay. "Abb, Abb, Abb," she said, touching the corner of her glasses. She emitted a long luxurious sigh. "I just couldn't take it any longer, that's all."

He ordered an extra dry Absolut Vodka Martini. "Take what?"

"Your—your, oh I don't know, there's just so much—maybe too much of so little."

Abb said, "Take a shot," and glanced over Cleo's shoulder, "err, a stab, or, whatever."

"A short list?" Cleo said, with a circumspect light in her eyes.

"Yes—yes, that's it, a short kind of list."

"Let's see, it's your fastidiousness, your chauvinism, your egocentrism."

"Hardly. I like everything neat is all. I follow certain ideologies. I do hold a certain position in my world of self, as I might add, everyone should." He sampled his drink and moved his martini glass in line with the small bud vase on the table.

"What of obsessiveness?" Cleo said, angling her spoon away from her glass at a rakish angle.

"Never." He bit his lower lip and stared at the wayward spoon.

"Compulsiveness?" Cleo said.

A quizzical expression spread across Abb's face. He plucked at a piece of lint and brushed his shirt sleeve. "Ah—I don't think so."

"Possessiveness?" Cleo sipped her wine.

Abb massaged his Rolex. "Possession is nine tenths of the law, my dear."

"Fixations?"

"Mere syllables, mere syllables, three to be exact."

"What about—"

Abb held up his right hand. "Enough, I get the picture of what you are alluding to, but surely I'm not anywhere near that."

"I can no longer be a bowled gold fish with you behind the glass, magnified, scrutinizing everything, controlling everything, micro-managing everything," Cleo said.

Abb nudged his fork toward the linen napkin so that it was perfectly parallel. "OK, OK. I see where you're going with this, but really where *are* you coming from? Controlling? Me?"

"You're suffocating me, strangling me, choking me. Can't you see?" Cleo ran her fingers over her throat. "What about here?" Her hand caressed her décolletage.

"Cleo, Cleo, Cleo, I've never laid a hand on you. Ask anyone."

"My circle of friends will attest to that, Abb, and not in a good way. No hand held, no shoulder cupped, no help stepping from car to curb."

Abb pinched the bridge of his nose. "Got that, but I would like to believe that it might rather be a *tiny* nod to stifle, dancing around the *edge* of smother, an oblique *suggestion* of repression. Maybe a *minuscule* of suppression?"

Cleo frowned and looked down. "There was nothing that I could look forward to anymore, nothing but unending insipidness. A black abyss unraveling all around, thanks to you."

Abb said, "All right, but I want you to consider that uniformity can be a good thing. Similitude. I like similitude. It has a certainty to it, a consistent ring."

"My voice: a lonely cry—"

"...a wail! My God."

"Abb, I *do not* wail. The dark empty void of the universe was becoming my life. A spent meaningless existence. My Being, screaming a tormented syllogism." Cleo's knuckles turned white.

Abb probed at an olive in his drink. "Hyperbole?"

"I felt as though I was a hollow chrysalis—longing for the Big Bang. What did you just say?"

Abb held both hands up. Palms showing, fingers spread. "Understood, but surely not futile, not pointless, nor hollow, or worthless, I'm sure. It couldn't be all of that, but, then again... There's truth in cliché, fact in stereotype."

"Let me tell you how I *really* feel," Cleo said, escalating their point, counter-point.

"Good because I'm beginning to see the picture, Cleo."

"But, where do I begin with you, Abb? Do I begin at the beginning, or just at The College of the Bahamas University?"

"Maybe at Indiana University-Purdue University Fort Wayne where we met?" Abb said.

"Remember the song, *"Back Home in Indiana"*? The Indy 500, ye olde Brick Yard?"

"I hardly want to sift through the debris of that debacle," Cleo said.

"Right, your family, living right there—townies. Your brother—whatta guy."

"We're not addressing my family or your family for that matter, are we, Abb, unless you would like to go there, hmmm?"

"No, Cleo. Do not drag our Alma Mater through the mud. I have just too many fond memories of those eight years." He squeezed the edge of the tablecloth. "That school, those days, the dark and isolated library stacks… Truly it was a brilliant time for both of us, you, with your B.A., me with my B.S."

Abberhider sat back and thought, *well, maybe not really all of that*, but he had to regain some ground here, change the subject, say something to place himself in a better light. After all, they were on a higher plane than mere animals—well at least the two of them; he couldn't speak for the rest of the room—and they could agree to disagree at this disagreeable moment.

Cleo held her wine glass at a slight angle as she made the urbane plea for civility in the matter: everyone involved was a rational adult, this sort of thing happens every day, and we'll all probably end up being the best of friends once this rush of pheromones is over. Gosalvez was so wonderful. Cleo knew that once Abberhider got to know Gosalvez he'd feel the same way toward her as she did—well almost the same way and damn it he'd better keep it that way.

"No, she's not Arabian. She's Aruban—from Aruba, in the Caribbean. There is a difference, you know." Cleo added. Piercing and tattooing had taken on a life of their own with the general public and with Gosalvez in particular. He should find himself warming to them if he wanted the two of them in his life at all.

"But, the question in my mind, Cleo, is what comes next?"

"We're leasing a penthouse near the lake…"

"I meant after the tats, piercings, gauging, branding?" Abb said.

"Oh that. Why? Do you want to make a killing on it? Be ahead of the wave? Work on some venture capital? That sort of thing?"

"I want to be modern, avant-garde. post-modern-contemporary, too. I don't want to be left behind—oh, and Stan and Ollie shouldn't be either."

"Please, leave Stan and Ollie out of this," Cleo said. "I don't want an ugly child custody battle erupting with them stuck in the middle."

"I know what can happen with kids being pulled this way and that. It's in the newspapers and tabloids all the time, especially in Hollywood," Abb said.

"But we're nowhere near Hollywood or any other wood for that matter," Cleo said, taking a sip of wine.

"But, are we talking folly, maybe Follywood?" Abb stole a quick glance over Cleo's shoulder. For a moment he couldn't take his eyes off her as their meeting's finale swirled near the periphery of his mind. He felt that he had to end on some kind of higher ground.

The other woman, that *Gostoavethz*, fondled a black cigarillo not even paying attention to them. Her right eye darted through the restaurant, touching on every architectural element, other tables, the female Maitre d'—while the left eye bore into the ceiling. Didn't she feel odd sitting alone with only her tweets?

Cleo had told Gosalvez they must take the BMW, that he, Abberhider, would worry if they had less than dependable transportation, the transit system being as dangerous and unreliable as it was. The two of them certainly weren't stooping so low as to be mere taxi fare, let alone bus steerage. I mean, how disgusting would that be?

Cleo shared that she and Gosalvez had met at a meeting protesting development of senior assisted living on the old Durante Ranch adjacent to the Regional Watershed Trust. They had gone from love of planet, to love of environment, to love of body parts within a matter of heartbeats. Cleo described Gosalvez as so full of life, so open to new pleasures and adventures, so spontaneous, so fresh, so depressed—so full of guilt and self-loathing. "She embraces all of humanity and wants everyone to have a life of simple comforts. She wants me to experience my full potential as a post, post-modern woman." Cleo leaned forward in her chair, emphasizing,

"Not being restricted, constricted, or predicted. You, on the other hand, Abb, like being restricted by your own constraints, predicted by your pre-requisites, and especially constricted as in uptight—we might be polar op-posites."

He said, "That's cold, but what about the big picture? Where is this pethous... uh, penthouse? Where is she staying?"

"Oh, Abb. I'm keeping her in the trunk of the car, of course," Cleo said.

In earnest, Abb balanced on the front legs of his chair. He rested his forearm on the edge of the table. "What will the Country Club think? What about Ollie and Stan? Your parents, if they call at all—when they ask, what should I tell them?"

Cleo studied his elbow on the table and arched on eyebrow, admonishing him for his uncouth mannerism. "Girls just want to have fun, so they say. And tell mother to please mail my see-through sport lingerie that I left at her timeshare last weekend."

Abb dropped his arm to his lap and drained his martini with his other hand. Cleo rose from her chair, swept toward the doorway with the other woman trooping behind her, leaving him with a mouth full of swirling liquor and a piece of olive stuck between his teeth.

Unable to locate a toothpick, and holding a napkin over his mouth, he caught up with them as they stepped toward the curb and the BMW.

"I'll be in touch," Cleo said, glancing over the top of the car at him.

Mute, Abberhider stood working his tongue against his teeth. Then they were gone, leaving him standing at the gutter.

In the taxicab on his way home from the train station Abberhider ruminated on what New Year's Eve might have in store for him with Cleo gone. He would probably do nothing more than switch channels between New York's big ball and the L.A. mob scene. All the same, Abb felt an enticement to consider some self-reinvention, but hadn't broken his habit of putting all the sections of the newspaper in order on the train, folding it for the next passenger, and placing the paper on the empty seat beside him. He made sure that the headline could be read as in the vending machine. If his eyes settled on a piece of lint dangling from another commuter's jacket as they stood in the aisle next to him, he would remove a small pair of tweezers from his inside suit pocket and pluck the speck from the material as the 5:10 clanged into the station.

He still focused on the "15 minute only" parking spaces looking for Cleo and fantasized her being there to pick him up in their new BMW. The third parking stall where she had parked for so many years remained empty, or worse, it was now occupied by a stranger waiting for someone else.

***

Cleo's most recent telephone message said that she'd decided to abandon red-meat, mall-crawl consumerism, squash lessons, and charity auctions. She had become a vegan and was now a member of the Harvest Temple and he, Abberhider, had no idea how wonderful living had become for them, that life was so much more than Corporate and Club. Oh, the demons, the demons. Her eyes had been opened and now she truly felt the burden of her family being carnivores, their guilt weighing heavily on her palate; her resolve had been steeled by eating only plant food from the Veldt, thereby reducing the footprint between her Being and Earth. She referred to it as her One-Stop Shopping Plan.

As he returned her telephone call, Abb couldn't get the phrase, "One-Shop Stopping" out of his mind. He settled into his favorite chair, intent on setting a certain scene for himself, the better to cope. He wouldn't say anything to dissuade her, though.

"You know, Abberhider, feeding and breeding like animals is not all there is to life," Cleo said. "Gosalvez and I are stepping away from the herd mentality with restored commitment."

He hoped that didn't mean flower power in the worst sense of the word as in two stomachs and methane.

"Just the other day," she said, "I was holding Gosalvez's hand: she was distraught, FIFA Cup you understand, and I reassured her that we were in this together. Only with unequivocal support would we be able to refrain from back-sliding into hamburger and pork sausage."

"FIFA? What's a FIFA, Cleo?"

"Oh, Abb, you *must* get out more. Federation Internationale de Football Association. And the women's world cup was established in '91. Soccer to you…"

Humbled, Abb could only think to say, "Her hand? I mean, all of it?" There was silence on the other end of the line. Recovering quickly, he said, "I realize that you're in an intimate relationship. Do your parents approve of it?" Girls gotta to do what girls gotta do flashed through his mind. Where had he heard that? What did it mean? Did it mean anything?

"I have to be me," she said.

As though any of us could be anyone else, he mused. He'd like to try that—being Mr. Anyone Else. Get rid of his thinning mouse-brown hair and shake off his butt that was becoming as wide as his shoulders. "Listen, I've been going over things—past things—rethinking, maybe I do have, or have had, some of those peccadilloes that you mentioned. Ollie and Stan miss you—I miss you. Some things were done wrong, I admit it. I see certain things more clearly, differently—Cleo, are you there?" He thought he heard heavy breathing on the other end of the line.

"What? Oh sure, just had to put cotton balls between my toes—pedicure—go on."

"Have you heard anything that I've said, for chrissake?" he stared at Ollie. Ollie folded one paw over the other and hid both of them with his head.

"Of course… and don't use rude language in front of Stan and Ollie. Tell them that I miss them terribly."

Then Abb asked again what her family thought about her current life style. Cleo said that her mother refused to send the peek-a-boo lingerie to her and never asked how Gosalvez was doing, which Mother pronounced "Gotsalivaz". Cleo could never forgive her mother for such an insult. Mailing her play things couldn't cost more than a few dollars and Cleo hadn't even demanded that the package be insured.

Before saying goodbye, Cleo added, "If Gosalvez's quarterly trust fund check from Aruba is late again, the postal service being so disgraceful, our lifestyle will have to be adjusted."

Abb pictured both of them hunkered down at a stoplight, cardboard sign in hand, without so much as a squeegee or water bottle. He ran his tongue over his lower lip before biting down. Stanley pursed his mouth and whined.

Waves of vindictiveness didn't wash over Abberhider anymore when the telephone rang and he'd stop raking the autumn leaves to listen to Cleo's litany about late checks.

"It's good to have someone like Gosalvez to talk with, share with," she said.

"Yes, I've found that," Abb said.

"You—you have someone—?"

"Yes, I've been getting help to see me through."

"Who?"

"Uh—a professional."

"Oh, a shrink type, huh?"

"He's very helpful."

"That's good, Abb. You need it. Have I heard of him?"

"I don't think so…"

"What's his name?"

"Maurice—"

"European, huh? They're the best. All that Freud, Jung, Austrian stuff."

"I didn't exactly mean—"

"No, that's good, Abb, that's good. You have to be a good father to Stan and Ollie," she said, hanging up.

"But, it's not for Ollie and Stan—they like me—put up with me the way I am," he shouted into the dead line and caught Ollie's wrinkled brow out of the corner of his eye.

* * *

It was a Friday night and Maurice's taxi brought Abb home. Back inside from scooping up after Ollie and Stan, he stopped on his way through the kitchen, to tear off February's calendar page showing the *Tres riches heures du Duc de Berry* by the Limbourg Brothers. He eased into his Strata Lounger, and was reading the comics in the evening paper while Mrs. Stouffer slaved in the microwave concocting a surprise for him.

The telephone jangled. "I'll get it," he said, as the dogs picked up their ears.

The voice on the other end of the line inquired, "Abberhider?" The voice seemed vaguely familiar, yet Abb couldn't quite place it. "This is Gosalvez."

"Of course, of course it is. I'd know your voice anywhere," Abb said. "It's been so long. How is your body art coming along: the tats, the piercing, the hang-me-downs in the ears and more private places?"

A long silence ensued between them, before, "I'm fine—doing well. Well not exactly fine…" A rhythmic tapping sound came through the phone and settled into his ear.

Gosalvez's long fingers jumped to mind. "Can you believe this weather we're having? I mean, can you believe it?" Abb said.

Gosalvez hesitated. "Abberhider… I was wondering… have you heard from Cleo?"

Abb rubbed Ollie's ear. No, the last he'd heard from either of them was when he received their card in December from Aruba. The shocking Caribbean colors hadn't disturbed him. The ridiculous photograph of the two women dancing across the card holding Christmas lights in lieu of bathing suits that spelled "Marry Christmas on One Happy Island" didn't bother him either. Although, he wished Cleo had convinced Gosalvez to shave her legs.

The thing that had galled him was the fact that the first stamp, the one with the blue Hairstreak Butterfly, had been smeared, while the second stamp, a yellow and blue background number with Revlon-Red sun was attached as if it was scaffolding in a Harold Lloyd comedy film. Anyway, it was probably the damn mailman—mail person—in the post office. Someone had peeled off the last stamp on the envelope so that now he'd never know what it looked like. God only knew how many people would foul the thing as it passed through their hands as it was. He could only imagine the colors, the interplay between forms, and the lettering of the tableau.

Gosalvez said, "I found a note when I came home tonight. I think that Cleo left with some sonofabitch from Chiapas that she's been hiding under the bed."

"Under her bed?"

"In her closet, in a sublet, in a apartment somewheres, numb-nuts. I could kill myself. She took our classic Jaguar and I'm worried. If anything happens to her—I'm talking about the car, here. We named it 'Maggs.' I'll…"

"Chiapas?"

"Mexico, dimmy."

"Of course, south of the border, down…"

"If you could let me know… Here's my cell phone number, my Facebook address, my—"

"Too much information," Abb said. He did agree to contact Gosalvez if he did hear anything from Cleo. Since Gosalvez was in the dark concerning Cleo's whereabouts. What would she tell Cleo's brother in Muncie, Indiana, if he called asking how things were going with the two of them after all, he was Pentecostal.

Then he assured her that it couldn't possibly happen twice: referring not to the way Cleo had left him, but to the travesty she and Cleo had suffered with the BMW. The two of them had parked near the catch basin of the reservoir one sultry evening and proceeded to get busy with each other. The recriminations suddenly erupted between the women as to who had released the emergency brake—was it Gosalvez's heavy boot spur or Cleo's stiletto heel? Cleo swore she'd put the car in park, not in neutral. Gosalvez could only recall that she'd wanted to park.

They had struggled to stop the car from careening backward, the heavy missile rocketing across the grass and into the lake, coming to rest in the pristine drinking water. Both of them starring at the mud, gasoline and oil oozing around them as the vehicle settled next to the "No Trespassing under Penalty of…" sign.

The Watershed Trust that the two of them had so vehemently defended against all enemies, had sued them for their little indiscretion—holding them libel, and for what? It had been an accident, as Cleo and Gosalvez had maintained all through the proceedings.

Their insurance company had refused to pay and the fiasco had dragged on for nine months. The nasty lawsuit from the Water District, the court appearances, money, time, and energy lost. The public sideshow resulted in a lawsuit they had brought against their lawyer for his nonsupport. Shortly afterward, the two women were forced by economic necessity to move, in disgrace, out to the Avenues.

The aroma of Mrs. Stouffer's Salisbury Dinner drifted in from the kitchen. Abb imagined Mrs. Stouffer putting her arms around his shoulders, saying, "Dinner's ready. Who was that on the phone?" Gazing out of the window, a light snow bussing the glass, he would answer. Oh, that—that was just some sales pitch, presumably from a soul mate of the recently departed.

He would again try to sort things out, not yet ready to take Maurice's advice and stop by the singles bar on his way home from work—hell, he didn't even do that before he met Cleo. What would it be like now? The music from Star Wars' Mos Eisley Cantina played in his head, the odd little ditty streaming in his ear loop.

***

Now, Abb doesn't let things take care of themselves, which they never did. On the other hand, that's exactly what they did—*she* did.

During his commute he tossed aside each section of the newspaper as he finished reading it, letting it fall where it might on the floor, and stepped across the ink and pulp when he reached his station. This alone freed him up. After doing it a few times, he knew that was not who he was either and struck what he hoped was a happy medium of leaving the paper in disarray on the seat beside him as he exited.

Minutia didn't seem so important anymore, although Abb did notice two white hairs on Stan's forehead the other day and immediately ran into the bathroom to examine his own eyebrows and chest. He reminded himself that there were more imperative issues to deal with. He made sure to call the city library concerning volunteering for the annual book sale. Clean up the Rivers and Shoreline Day didn't slip by without him being there. He offered his neighbor some flowers from his greenhouse and asked Maurice's guidance concerning repairing the jalousie windows on the three-season porch. At the end of the day, after walking the dogs, he returned home to Mrs. Stouffer, a warm fire, and an Irish coffee.

The two dogs lolled next to Abb while he sang along to the Oldies but Goodies song tracks. Stan laid his muzzle on the rug. Ollie scratched himself with his hind leg. Abb's shoulder muscles relaxed.

The doorbell sang its five chords, the dogs jumped and rushed to the threshold. Abb turned on the portico light and opened the door.

"Hi," she said.

They studied each other.

"Hi," he said. "Some surprise—you—here. Come in, come in. Don't stand out there in the cold. What brings you to this neighborhood? It's good to see you, Cleo."

"Oh, I was just following bread crumbs." She bent, petted both dogs, kissed their foreheads, and ruffled their ears.

Abb stretched to see if she had a large suitcase that might hide someone behind her. His eyes darted over her shoulder, checking for "Maggs" the Jag, but saw nothing. "Come in, come in..."

Cleo moved inside as Stan and Ollie pranced in front of her. He looked at her. She looked at him. "The house looks nice, Abb," she said, noticing the dogs' toys strewn on the floor, the magazines, and the half-empty cup of coffee.

"So do you, Cleo, so do you." He took in the pink crop top beneath her puffy jacket, ready-to-wear skinny jeans and *All Stars* running shoes.

Abb made another Irish coffee and they began talking about how good it was to make it through winter. Now that it was March, the weather should break. Cleo pointed out that his slippers looked a bit chewed on. Stanley hid behind the sofa. Abb laughed it off. Different subjects popped up more or less from free association. Cleo rummaged in the bottom of her purse, found some beef jerky, and divided it between the four of them. With familiar ease they slipped into new avenues of discussion. De-Ja-Vu was not a stranger as they chatted—they even snickered.

"I thought of you the other day when I picked up sticky buns and ketchup for dinner," Cleo said.

"And you came to mind when I returned a dead basil plant to the nursery and they told me the receipt was from the grocery store," Abb said.

He offered to show her around, after all, he'd been able to DIY a bit—some paint touch-up here, a different sofa pillow there. A large pink ceramic pig squatted in the kitchen stuffed with dog biscuits. A TV tray folded at the ready next to his Strata-Lounger. She noted the blank monthly calendar—a worn and creased business card, reading "Taxi Service" with its scrawled phone number.

He noticed the wisps of hair on Cleo's neck as they walked up the stairs and she turned her head to gaze at the living room, below. The fine pattern of lines held in her skin as she turned her attention to the bedroom. Abb's eyes rested on her profile.

He recalled when they first met at the university in Indiana. Studying on the grass, she had glanced up as he returned from the grocery store and tried riding his skateboard down the concrete steps. The clatter announced his failure, as beer cans, pie tins, and dental floss exploded everywhere like a Roman candle on the Fourth of July.

Their discovery of Stan at the animal shelter, the pup catching Cleo's chin with his muzzle resulting in three stitches at Urgent Care, her red badge of courage.

With a wistful smile Abb recounted the trip home from Emergency when they found Ollie, trying to pull Chinese take-away out of a garbage can in the alley next to Giorgio's Left Bank Restaurant.

A new California King bed hung from the ceiling on tapered brushed aluminum rods. The two dogs walked back and forth beneath the frame. Abberhider flicked on the bedside mood lights. Cleo didn't seem to notice as he deftly turned the old framed Cruise Mecca itinerary with her farewell note to him toward the wall so the red handwriting was hidden. A yellow Post-It note covered the gouged picture of Valerie, their tour guide that Cleo had pummeled. He didn't feel the need for beating himself up at the moment.

Cleo ran her fingers over the aubergine-color satin sheets, sat on the bed, and crossed her legs. She let one shoe dangle off the ball of her foot, flexing her toes—seeming to test the inner spring mattress. Abb thought that he might soon be breaking some bad news to poor Mrs. Stouffer, but then that's life.

About the Author

Lee Holt currently lives and works in the San Francisco Bay Area. Raised in the Midwest, his stories draw from the rich fabric of these two unique regions of the country.

Necessary Reflections is the first compilation of short stories from this author. He is currently writing and illustrating a children's book.